MISSISSIPPI!

The fifteenth unforgettable volume
in the WAGONS WEST series—
all new rip-roaring adventures of America's
boldest frontiersmen and women who would fight
for their ideals of freedom and justice
against any evil . . . at any odds.

★★★★★★★★★★★★★★★★★★★★★★★★★★★★★★★★★★★★★

WAGONS WEST

MISSISSIPPI!

AMERICA'S MIGHTIEST RIVER SWEPT
THEM TO DANGER, DESIRE,
AND A NEW CLASH WITH DESTINY.

TOBY HOLT—
A man brave enough to face any peril, strong enough
to fight any enemy, his new mission took him
dangerously far from his cherished family
and lethally close to the West's most
powerful criminal mastermind.

MILLICENT RANDALL—
A prisoner to passions that have carried her to
the limits of shame and into the arms of a
villain she cannot escape.

KARL KELLERMAN—
An ex-lawman with a knave's cunning and no
conscience, he takes whatever and whomever
he wants with violence and death.

WALLACE DUGALD—
A good man horribly wronged by a trusted friend,
he would sell his soul for revenge.

★★★★★★★★★★★★★★★★★★★★★★★★★★★★★★★★★★★★★

★★★★★★★★★★★★★★★★★★★★★★★★★★★★★★★★★★★★★★★

EDWARD BLACKSTONE—
A gentleman who hides a fist of steel in his velvet
glove, he must put duty before the woman he loves.

TOMMIE HARDING—
A courageous young woman whose dreams of
happiness are doomed unless she can save
her fiancé from certain death.

KUNG LEE—
Master of a Chinese Tong, absolute power has
made him untouchable; absolute evil makes
him terrifyingly cruel.

DOMINO—
A sinner not a saint in New Orleans, he's a mob
boss who believes in honor among thieves . . . and
in the word of Whip Holt's son.

MARTHA—
A woman so sensually beautiful that even the most
faithful man might risk his marriage to taste the
sweetness of her charms.

★★★★★★★★★★★★★★★★★★★★★★★★★★★★★★★★★★★★★★★

Bantam Books by Dana Fuller Ross
Ask your bookseller for the books you have missed

WAGONS WEST ★ FIFTEENTH IN A SERIES

MISSISSIPPI!

DANA FULLER ROSS

Created by the producers of
White Indian, Children of the
Lion, Stagecoach, and Saga of the
Southwest.

Chairman of the Board: Lyle Kenyon Engel

BANTAM BOOKS
TORONTO · NEW YORK · LONDON · SYDNEY · AUCKLAND

MISSISSIPPI!

A Bantam Book / June 1985

Produced by Book Creations, Inc.
Chairman of the Board: Lyle Kenyon Engel

ISBN 0-553-24976-2

Published simultaneously in the United States and Canada

PRINTED IN THE UNITED STATES OF AMERICA

H   0 9 8 7 6 5 4 3 2

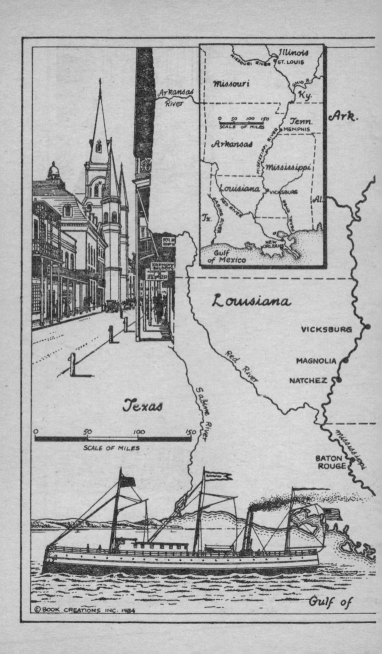

Arkansas River

Illinois
MISSOURI RIVER ST. LOUIS

Missouri

OHIO R.

Ky.

Ark.

SCALE OF MILES
0 50 100 150

Tenn.
MEMPHIS

MISSISSIPPI RIVER

Arkansas

Mississippi

Louisiana

VICKSBURG

Al.

Tx.

RED RIVER

SABINE RIVER

PEARL RIVER

NEW ORLEANS

Gulf
of Mexico

POLICE
DEPT.

PATRICK'S
SALOON

Louisiana

Red River

VICKSBURG

MAGNOLIA

NATCHEZ

Texas

Sabine River

SCALE OF MILES
0 50 100 150

Mississippi

BATON
ROUGE

© BOOK CREATIONS INC. 1984

Gulf of

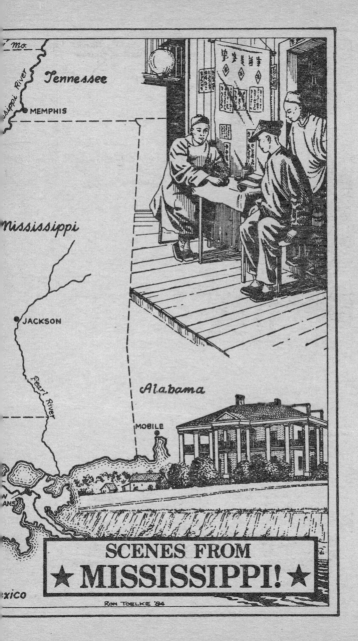

Tennessee

MEMPHIS

Mississippi

JACKSON

Pearl River

Alabama

MOBILE

Mo.

SCENES FROM
★ MISSISSIPPI! ★

RON TOELKE '84

★ ★ WAGONS WEST ★ ★

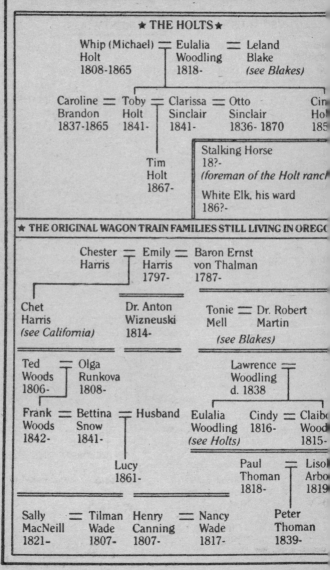

★ THE HOLTS ★

Whip (Michael) = Eulalia = Leland
Holt   Woodling   Blake
1808-1865   1818-   *(see Blakes)*

Caroline = Toby = Clarissa = Otto   Cin
Brandon   Holt   Sinclair   Sinclair   Ho
1837-1865 1841- 1841-   1836- 1870   185

Tim
Holt
1867-

Stalking Horse
18?-
(foreman of the Holt ranch

White Elk, his ward
186?-

★ THE ORIGINAL WAGON TRAIN FAMILIES STILL LIVING IN OREGO

Chester = Emily = Baron Ernst
Harris   Harris   von Thalman
          1797-   1787-

Chet   Dr. Anton   Tonie = Dr. Robert
Harris   Wizneuski   Mell   Martin
(see California) 1814-   *(see Blakes)*

Ted   = Olga   Lawrence =
Woods   Runkova   Woodling
1806-   1808-   d. 1838

Frank = Bettina = Husband   Eulalia   Cindy = Claibc
Woods   Snow   Woodling   1816-   Wood
1842-   1841-   *(see Holts)*   1815-

Lucy   Paul = Lisol
1861-   Thoman Arbo
                             1818-   1819

Sally = Tilman   Henry = Nancy   Peter
MacNeill Wade   Canning Wade   Thoman
1821-   1807-   1807-   1817-   1839-

★ ★ FAMILY TREE ★ ★

★ THE BLAKES, MARTINS, AND BRENTWOODS ★

ualia ═ Leland ═ Cathy
oodling Holt   Blake   van Ayl
ee Holts)   1804-   1814-1865

onie ═ Dr. Robert   Sam ═ Claudia
ell   Martin   Brentwood   Humphries
314-   1798-   1797-   1809-

le ═ Rob ═ Beth   Susanna ═ Andrew Jackson
ton Martin   Blake   Fulton   Brentwood
46- 1841-   1841-1869   1837-   1839-

ank Blake   Cathy   Samuel
dopted)   Martin   Brentwood
50-   1869-   1866-

★ IN NEW ORLEANS ★

nmie   Edward   Jean-Pierre   Millicent   Jim
ding   Blackstone   Gautier   Randall   Randall
0-   1840-   1843-   1845-   *(see below)*
iah Harding's
ughter)

★ LIVING IN IDAHO ★

Jim   Pamela
Randall ═ Drake
1843-   1841-

★ LIVING IN CALIFORNIA ★

t ═ Clara Lou   Wong ═ Wing
ris   Hadley   Ke   Mei Lo
2-   1823-   1809-   1835-

ther ═ Danny   Ginny (Virginia) ═ Hector
Gregor Taylor   Dobbs   Mullins
8-   1823-   1814-   1804-

Woods   Melissa ═ Rick ═ Elisabeta   Child   Child
or   Austin   Miller   Manuel   1849-   1851-
0-   1824-   1815-   1823-1849

Child   Child
1853-   1854-

CREATIONS INC. 1984   RON TOELKE '84

MISSISSIPPI!

I

The huge stern paddle wheel turned slowly as the great river steamer made its way steadily down the broad, placid waters of the Mississippi. The mighty mile-wide river had long been the principal thoroughfare for moving the produce of the American heartland to market.

Millicent Randall was standing at the prow of the ship. On both sides of the river, she could see enormous amounts of activity as the grain, timber, cotton, and vegetables that were in demand throughout the United States and Europe were loaded on the wharves to be sent to market. The commerce on the Mississippi, she realized, was one of the principal reasons that the United States, with the debilitating Civil War behind her, was becoming a great nation in the 1870s. America truly had been blessed by nature.

The sun was warm. The breeze rippled gently through the soft folds of Millicent's thin, clinging

dress, and even a casual observer would have noted
from the way that the wind pressed the fabric against
the young woman's ripe, full figure that she was
wearing nothing underneath her garment. To a lady
of 1870, Millicent's attire was shocking, but the truth
of the matter was that Millicent, once a prim, proper
young woman from Baltimore, who composed music
and played the flute, no longer qualified as a lady.

Without her knowledge, Millicent had been fed
a Gypsy potion made from mind-altering, central
European mushrooms, and her life had been dramati-
cally changed. Aroused erotically for the first time in
her life by the gambler/businessman Luis de Cordova,
who had used the potion in order to get her to do his
bidding, she had begun to dress and act in a provocative manner. She had gone off with de Cordova to
St. Louis, and on the way he had treated her badly,
using her as bait to engage men in card games—with
Millicent as the prize—and then cheating the card
players so that he amassed a small fortune. Subsequently he had paid for his dishonesty with his life.

Her new companion, Sergeant Karl Kellerman,
who had recently resigned his position with the St.
Louis constabulary, was taking her to New Orleans.
Dazzled by the brown-haired, provocative young
woman—who combined an air of good breeding with
startling sensuality—he had lavished many gifts on
her.

Kellerman had indicated to Millicent that he
liked her unusual attire and heavy use of makeup;
she was so much in love with him that she dressed

and used cosmetics to please him. But whenever she was alone and knew she was not going to be seeing Karl for a number of hours, she became more like her old self, wearing modest clothes and using very little makeup. She had no way of knowing that the recent change in her was due to the fact that the effects of the mind-altering drug de Cordova had used to control her had worn off.

Looking at the cat's-eye sapphire ring she wore on her right hand, Millicent considered herself the most fortunate woman alive. Karl had given her the ring in Memphis on their journey south, and she had no idea that it was tainted with the blood of its previous owner. No, Millicent only knew that her troubles were behind her, that her future was as bright as the river sparkling in the rays of the sun. Everything about Karl and the journey enchanted her, including the fine foods and wines that they were served at every meal, their lavish suite on the ship, and their frequent lovemaking.

When the stern-wheeler put into the old cotton port of Natchez, where a concerted rebuilding campaign was eliminating the scars left by Civil War fighting, Millicent went ashore with Karl and delighted in every moment of the experience. She and Karl made a tour of the city and then went to a fashionable restaurant on the riverfront to dine. Millicent was in her glory. Wearing one of the new gowns he had given her, a low-necked dress of crimson velvet with a matching broad-brimmed hat, she was the object of all eyes. Millicent glowed, aware of the stir she was creating, and the large, well-built, dark-blond-haired Karl, jauntily smoking a long cigar, seemed highly pleased by the fuss that resulted.

Under the circumstances, it was easy and almost inevitable for Millicent to daydream. She had no doubt that she and Karl would marry after they reached New Orleans, their destination, and her mind dwelled lovingly on the details of the luxurious life she would lead as his wife. She was in no way dismayed by the fact that he had not proposed marriage to her: Her daydreams were based on anything but reality.

The riverboat reached the great port city of New Orleans slightly over two days later. In effect the post–Civil War capital of the South, New Orleans was unique among American cities. Tied up along her Mississippi waterfront were the barges that brought the cotton bales of the South, the wheat of Minnesota, Dakota, and Kansas, and the corn of Iowa and Illinois to the city for transfer to the great ships that would carry the produce to the Atlantic seaboard states, to the Caribbean and to Europe, and even to Asia. Manufacturing plants were rising faster than anyone could count them, and a variety of industries was adding to the city's economic strength.

New Orleans was a fascinating cultural mixture of France and Spain, whose colony she once had been, and of the old American West. The restaurants catered to all tastes, with some as rough-and-tumble as frontier saloons and others as sophisticated and unique as any in America. Many of the shops were elegant and expensive, and even the gambling halls and brothels could be almost indescribably lavish.

Millicent was dazzled by New Orleans and its atmosphere. Now, seventy-two hours after her arrival in the Queen City, she was sitting in her dressing room in the suite that Kellerman had rented for them in the Louisiana House, one of the best hotels in town, trying to curb her sense of excitement. She gave in to the ministrations of Effie, the pretty, light-skinned black maid whom Kellerman had hired for her through the hotel. Effie was busy with a comb and brush, arranging Millicent's long brown hair, and the young woman marveled at the efficiency of the maid.

"Every time I go anywhere in this town," Millicent said, "and it doesn't matter if it's a restaurant or a dress shop or where it is, I'm just astonished by the people I see. I've spent the past few years in the mountains and small towns of the West, and I grew up in Baltimore, which is a large city in its own right, but nowhere have I seen women as beautiful as there are on the streets of New Orleans!"

"There ain't none that's prettier than you, Mrs. Kellerman," Effie replied with great sincerity. She had learned that her new mistress was not married to Karl Kellerman but nevertheless did her the honor of referring to her as the wife of her employer.

Millicent smiled and shook her head. "They have a quality that I lack—a kind of sophistication."

"You'd never know it from the way you look and act, ma'am," Effie said flatly. "Now hold still while I pin up your hair." She worked in silence for a moment, then went on, "You know that sad-faced young gent'man we keep seeing all over town? You handle him just right, the way you pretend he don't exist. No New Orleans woman could handle him any better."

Millicent was embarrassed. For the past three days, whenever she had left the Louisiana House, she had been followed at a distance by a well-dressed, clean-cut young man, whom Effie had identified as Jean-Pierre Gautier, a wealthy young New Orleans heir who had lost a sickly wife about a year earlier. He seemed to be much taken by Millicent, and certainly it could not be accidental that he appeared everywhere she went, nodding to her politely and wishing her good morning or good afternoon.

She had handled the situation by ignoring him, for she was afraid Karl would become highly jealous and even violent if she acknowledged the stranger in any way. To her surprise, however, Karl had displayed only indifference to young Gautier's interest in her. She found it hard to understand or appreciate Kellerman's reasoning; apparently, he was confident that he already had possession of her and was strangely willing to let another man seek her company. Furthermore, as he had told her, he had no desire to become involved in unpleasantness with the wealthy, socially prominent Gautier family.

Effie pushed a pair of white egret feathers into Millicent's dark, upswept hair, then examined her own handiwork critically.

"Are you sure you don't want me to come shopping with you this afternoon, ma'am?" Effie asked.

Stepping into the dress that the maid held for her, Millicent replied emphatically, "I'm very positive. After all, this is the day your little boy is coming from his grandmother's house to visit you, and I know how eager you are to see him."

Effie was deeply touched. She worked for a living because of her need to support her young child, who meant everything to her, and she was touched by the consideration of her new employer, who had remembered her casual statement that her son was visiting that day. "Thank you, ma'am, and God bless you," she murmured.

"Nonsense," Millicent replied briskly. "That's the very least I can do for you." She examined herself in the mirror, then picked up her handbag. "How do I look?"

"Just perfect, ma'am! That Mr. Gautier is going to swoon when he sees you today."

Millicent joined in the maid's laugh. "If you happen to see Mr. Kellerman before you leave," she said, "would you tell him for me that I'll meet him back here at five o'clock this afternoon?"

"Yes, ma'am, I'll tell him."

"Be sure you give your son a hug and kiss from me," Millicent said as she left the suite.

Effie began to clean up the dressing table and to hang up clothes that Millicent had not chosen to wear. The maid told herself she was fortunate not only to have found employment that paid sufficient wages to support her son and herself but also to have found a mistress as kind as Millicent. In these days when jobs were not easy to find, necessity had forced many of her friends to seek work in brothels.

Finishing her chores quickly, Effie was about to depart when the door to the sitting room opened and Karl Kellerman's bulk filled the frame.

Six feet three inches tall, with broad shoulders and a barrellike chest, he stood now with his thumbs hooked in the belt that held his twin .44 caliber pistols.

Effie saw him eyeing her attractive face and figure. She had never been alone with him like this, and she was distinctly uncomfortable. "You just missed madam by a few minutes, sir," she said, trying to conceal her nervousness. "She said she'll meet you back here about five o'clock. She's gone shopping."

"Thanks, Effie," he drawled, continuing to eye her speculatively. He was grateful to be free of Millicent that long. The woman's cloying manner and her ingenuous excitement over being in New Orleans were beginning to get on his nerves. A scant hour ago, at the restaurant where he had lunch he had met a stunning blonde who would be available, he knew, and he also had his eye on a provocatively seductive redhead who worked at the establishment where he had eaten the day before. Right now, he had a craving for this mulatto, which should be easy enough to fulfill.

"Well," he said, "both of us have some time to

kill. What do you say we kill it together?" He crooked one long finger and beckoned to her.

Effie's blood ran cold. Not only did Kellerman hold no appeal to her, but far more important, she had no intention of repaying Millicent's loyalty by cheating on her. She made no move.

Kellerman chuckled, reached for her lazily, and pulling her close, began to paw her buttocks with his free hand.

Effie resorted to an old trick and pretended to relax. Then, when he eased his grip, she suddenly wrenched away from him.

Kellerman was surprised for the moment but was in no way disturbed. He could handle any woman.

He reached into a waistcoat pocket, withdrew a twenty-dollar gold piece, and carelessly flipped it to the maid. Effie caught the coin and identified it. Her mind immediately filled with thoughts of the clothing, food, and toys that the magnificent sum of twenty dollars—which represented two weeks' wages—could buy for her little son. She stood indecisively for a long moment as Kellerman's dark eyes seemed to bore into her. It occurred to her that it was even worth jeopardizing her job in order to have so much money all at once. Slowly she began to unbutton the blouse of her uniform, as Kellerman's triumphant chuckle rang in her ears.

Half an hour later, the nervous Effie dressed rapidly. She could hardly wait until she put distance between herself and the brute who had just made love to her with such callousness. "Please tell madam," she said, concealing her hate for him as best she could, "that I'm sorry I won't be seeing her again, but I quit the job here and now."

When Millicent returned to the suite several hours later, laden with packages from her afternoon of shopping, Kellerman, who was drinking a stiff bourbon and water in the parlor as he smoked a long cigar, told her that the maid had resigned and departed. Millicent was taken aback by the news. She had genuinely liked Effie and was surprised by her unexpected resignation. "Why did she leave?" she asked. "What did she say?"

"She said nothing," he lied. "She asked for her wages, which I paid, and she quit. You know the type. She's shiftless and has no sense of responsibility."

Still disappointed, Millicent couldn't help wondering how she could have misjudged the maid's character so badly.

The next morning, Karl left Millicent behind at their hotel suite, telling her he had to go on a little errand involving business. Millicent didn't know what his business was but knew better than to ask. She was content to spend the morning in bed, having been out with Karl until late the night before.

Now the former police sergeant walked slowly down the crowded street toward the New Orleans business district, taking in the sights of the city and enjoying his experience thoroughly. In all of his travels, never had he seen so many chic, stunningly attractive young women as there were in New Orleans. At a rough estimate, he guessed that there were ten beautiful girls in New Orleans for each one in St. Louis, where he had been a detective sergeant.

Certainly he had made the right move when he had resigned from the constabulary and had decided to make his fortune by his wits. And this was the city for him: a place where the pleasures of the flesh were available to men of means.

Karl did not regret having brought Millicent Randall to New Orleans with him, even though her support was costing him a small fortune. Her beauty was exceptional, making her the equal of any woman in New Orleans, and in addition, she was a passionate bed partner. But he was growing tired of her, and he couldn't help thinking how he would enjoy some new diversions, like that blonde and the redhead. He would have to devote himself to meeting these new women after he arranged a few business deals. Also, although he had other plans at the moment, he would would soon look in on his partner, Wallace Dugald, whom he had financed to open a bar near the waterfront the last time he was in New Orleans.

Turning a corner, Kellerman slowed his pace as he approached an inconspicuous, two-story building. On the ground floor was a modest greengrocer's shop with a variety of vegetables displayed in the bins outside on the wooden sidewalk. On the side of the building, a narrow wooden staircase rose to the second floor, and Karl mounted it slowly, halting when he entered a room off the landing. Two men with hard, expressionless faces sat reading the morning newspapers. They looked up at him searchingly, and he was quick to identify himself.

"I'm Kellerman," he said. "Domino sent for me."

One of the pair nodded and grunted. "All right," he said, "we'll relieve you of your pistol. While you're at it, you can leave the knife that you're carrying in the top of your boot out here, too. We'll take good care of your weapons until you leave."

Karl knew better than to argue with the guards and surrendered his weapons to them. One of them disappeared into a back room for a few moments. When he returned to the anteroom, he beckoned abruptly. "The boss will see you."

Karl followed him into a small, drab chamber at the second floor rear. There, seated behind a modest desk, was the gray-haired man who had earned his name because of his love for the game of dominoes. The general public had never heard of him, but he was known in certain circles as the most influential member of the underworld that thrived along the Mississippi River. The police of towns and cities along the great river had reason to believe that he was involved in a variety of activities, from grand larceny to prostitution, but they had absolutely nothing they could pin on him.

Domino's appearance belied his reputation. A pair of metal-rimmed spectacles rested on the bridge of his nose, his gray hair was neatly combed, and he was wearing a worsted, rust-colored suit. Those who did not know him invariably took him for a bookkeeper or some other minor functionary in the city's business world.

Waving a small, neatly manicured hand, Domino did not rise as he pointed his visitor to a chair on the far side of his desk. "Sit down, Kellerman, and I'll tell you why I sent for you," he said in a mild voice. Turning to the guard, Domino ordered him to leave the room so that the two men could speak in private.

Karl felt uneasy under Domino's careful scrutiny.

"I was interested," Domino said, "to learn of your resignation from the St. Louis constabulary. Surely you don't earn enough to live in the style to which you've accustomed yourself on your half interest in the saloon here."

Karl was not surprised to learn of Domino's awareness of his investment in a New Orleans bar. The gang leader made it his business to know everything about anyone engaging in any business in the South.

"I've had no specific plans to augment my income," he said, "but I was intending to look you up and pay you a visit. I can use some extra income these days."

Domino smiled vaguely. "I understand that you're traveling with a real beauty. Women are expensive." He did not pursue the point.

"Yes," Karl replied curtly. "She's expensive."

"I trust," Domino said, "you're not squeamish about assignments that you undertake?"

"Try me," Karl said. He did not intend to boast

that he was directly responsible for two recent deaths, of which Domino was probably well aware.

"I know your background," Domino told him, "and you're just the person to perform a job that has been waiting for the right man. Are you familiar with the Three-Two-One Club?"

Reluctant to reveal his ignorance, Karl shook his head.

"It's in an old Creole mansion on Jefferson Avenue," Domino said. "During the war it was converted into a private gaming club, and it's expanded since that time. Girls are available, of course, and they also serve meals. There is one large room for those who like to do a bit of gambling for high stakes. It's strictly a rich man's club. The security there is lax—surprisingly lax," Domino went on. "I stop in occasionally for an evening of cards myself, and I'm always astonished by the lack of protection. One experienced man who knows what he's doing can collect thousands of dollars in a properly staged holdup."

Karl's face was expressionless. "Sounds interesting," he said. "What's the fee?"

"Twenty percent of the first ten thousand you collect, and twenty-five percent of everything over that amount. Take it or leave it."

"Not so fast," Karl said. "What help will I get from you and from your organization?"

"Absolutely none," Domino told him coolly. "The haul will be so large that I'll automatically be suspected of having had a hand in the robbery. But I intend to turn the tables on the police and on the other gangs of New Orleans. I'm going to be a patron at the Three-Two-One on the night of the robbery, and I expect to be personally robbed and then treated exactly as you treat the other patrons."

"That's very clever of you," Karl said, his mind working quickly. He would be even more clever. Instead of taking all the risks and submitting himself to the dangers of the enterprise in return for a meager twenty or twenty-five percent of the spoils, he decided it would be far simpler and infinitely more satisfying to do away with Domino. Then he could keep the entire proceeds of the robbery for himself. If necessary, he would go into hiding until the repercussions of the affair blew over.

They parted amicably, with Karl retrieving his weapons from the outer office. When he reached the street, he began to walk back toward the Louisiana House, taking his time, going over his whole conversation with Domino. He had been right to come back to New Orleans, he reflected, and so far, he was in luck. He saw no reason his fortunes should change, and as soon as he accumulated enough money, he could have any girl that he wanted.

Pamela Randall sat before the open window of her second-floor bedchamber in the comfortable, spacious farmhouse and looked out at a familiar but beautiful scene. In the background, beyond the ranch that she and her husband owned, stood the impressive, rugged, snowcapped mountains that formed a vigilant, permanent guard over the Idaho Territory. The land stretched as far as the eye could see, and the pastures where the horses and cows grazed were lush and green beneath the warm June sun. The air that blew in from the mountains was crisp and dry. Truly, Pamela thought, she had never been in a region as lovely as this, not even in the rolling, verdant countryside of Sussex, England, where she had grown up.

Beautiful, aristocratic-looking—with her abundant wheat-colored hair piled on top of her head— Pamela was lost in thought as she looked out the window in the direction of the corral and caught a glimpse of her husband's foreman, Randy Savage, dismounting from his horse. Tall, rugged, sandy-haired, and very handsome, Randy had been the reason for Pamela's almost ruining her life. Having had little else to occupy her over the winter months— and intrigued because he was so different from the men she had known in her native England—Pamela had foolishly imagined herself in love with him. And Randy, greatly taken with Pamela's beauty and realizing the way she felt about him, had thought that he was in love with her, too.

Fortunately, their mutual common sense had asserted itself, and they had stepped back from the abyss in time. There was no harm done, and neither was any worse for the experience.

As Pamela continued to watch, another horseman entered the corral and dismounted. It was her husband, Jim Randall, a lean, hard, brown-haired veteran of the Civil War, who had lost an eye in the war and wore an eye patch that gave him an added touch of distinction. Jim had sufficient funds that he could have lived in comfort in his native Baltimore for the rest of his days, but it was typical of him to have come to the West, to have bought a ranch, and to have created a new and useful life for himself. Pamela had met Jim shortly after she arrived in the United States, and feeling it was time to settle down and put a stop to her carefree, coquettish ways, she had married him. Only recently, however, had she learned to appreciate Jim fully, and her heart was filled with love as she watched him.

Jim and Randy began talking. Watching them together, Pamela couldn't imagine how she could have thought herself in love with the foreman. Her husband was extraordinary.

The discussion in the corral was spirited but brief and ended in seeming agreement. Randy hurried off to the bunkhouse, and Jim entered the main dwelling, appearing in a few moments in his wife's bedchamber. "When I picked up the mail in Boise this morning," he said without preamble, "I found another letter from Edward that had just arrived." He handed her the letter, written on hotel stationery.

Edward Blackstone, a dashing, wealthy young Englishman who had been Pamela's next-door neighbor in rural Sussex, had originally traveled with her to America in order to see the country and to attend to business matters here. After Pamela had married Jim, Edward's cousin, Edward decided to travel from Fort Benton, Montana, to St. Louis by boat down the Missouri River because he sought the rich

experience. The letter related how he had encountered their mutual relative, Millicent Randall, traveling with Luis de Cordova, who, as it turned out, was
a crooked gambler. Edward had killed de Cordova,
who had tried to cheat him at cards, and the
Englishman had thought that Millicent was safe at
last.

But now, Edward said, Millicent had vanished in
St. Louis in the company of Sergeant Karl Kellerman,
who had left the constabulary there. Edward asked
for Jim's help, as well as that of any volunteers he
cared to bring with him to St. Louis, where Edward
and his fiancée, Tommie Harding, would await
reinforcements.

"What a shame to have found Millicent, only to
lose her again," Jim said, shaking his head. He and
Pamela had been shocked when his staid and reliable
cousin had sold her restaurant in Boise the previous
winter and had run off with de Cordova, and they
had been relieved when Edward wrote that he had
found her. But now Millicent's activities were more
shocking than ever, and Jim said, "This running away,
first with one man and then another, isn't at all like
her."

"It's possible there's a simple explanation for her
conduct," Pamela replied. "Perhaps the recognition
that men find her desirable has altered her personal-
ity and caused her to act foolishly."

"Quite possibly you're right," he said. "But whatever may be motivating her, I can't let Edward down.
I telegraphed him at his hotel in St. Louis to the

effect that I'll be leaving from Boise right away to catch the railroad in Ogden, Utah, and I should be arriving in St. Louis in two weeks' time. I've just spoken to Randy Savage, and he's going with me. Edward doesn't explain why he needs help, but the mere fact that he needs it is good enough for me. He doesn't explain either who this Tommie Harding is."

Pamela put a finger to her lips and pondered for a moment. "Do you remember, dear, just before Edward left Boise for Fort Benton to begin his trip down the Missouri, he told us he was going to sail on a ship of the Harding Line? Could it be that this Tommie Harding is the daughter of the ship's captain, the owner of the line? In any event, it appears that we're going to have a new relative one of these days."

"I hope," Jim said, "that you don't object to my going off to St. Louis to help Edward."

"Of course not!" Pamela told him. "Edward wouldn't ask for help unless he really needed it. We have no choice."

He nodded. "I was pretty sure you'd feel that way," he said, putting his arm around her. "I'll appoint an acting foreman to take charge of operations here at the ranch, and you know I'll come home as soon as I possibly can."

"Don't hurry on my account," Pamela replied. "I'll cope with things here. You stay with Edward for as long as necessary to solve this mystery about Millicent once and for all."

So Jim and Randy left the ranch that afternoon,

traveling by horseback to Ogden. They set an ardu-
ous pace for themselves and arrived in the bustling
railroad town some ten days later. Leaving their
horses at a local stable and wiring ahead to Edward
Blackstone, they boarded a Union Pacific train heading east and arrived in St. Louis less than forty-eight
hours later.

Edward and Tommie Harding were awaiting the
arrival of the train in St. Louis, and they greeted the
newcomers warmly. As always, Edward was impecca-
bly and expensively dressed in a tailor-made suit and
shirt with lace cuffs. His pencil-thin mustache was
neatly trimmed, as was his dark brown hair, and he
and the pert, blond-haired Tommie, who was wearing a plain but becoming blue dress, made a good-
looking couple. Jim quickly discovered that Tommie
was even more attractive, vivacious, and intelligent
than he had thought at first glance, and he was very
impressed by her.

Because of the presence of the carriage driver,
they said nothing about the mission that had brought
them all together. Instead, Edward explained how
he and Tommie had met and fallen in love and how
they had promised Tommie's father, who was indeed
the owner of the Harding Line, that they would wait
before getting married in order to be sure they were
right for each other. In the meantime, they were
traveling together, an unconventional arrangement
for an unmarried man and woman, but then Tommie
was far too independent-minded and free-spirited to
be considered conventional. What was more, Edward,

always the gentleman, saw to it that they slept in separate rooms when they registered at hotels.

When they reached the hotel, they made themselves comfortable in the living room of Edward's suite. There, Tommie handed Jim a clipping from a recent newspaper. "Read this," Edward said.

Jim read the news story from Memphis that told of the death of a gang leader there. The man, named Jason, had been found in his office, shot to death. It had been a suicide, the article said, but subsequently it had been revealed that one of his bodyguards also had died. No one knew the identity of the perpetrator of the crime or what the link was between the suicide and the murder, but it was speculated that the killer might have been an exceptionally tall and broad-shouldered man with dark blond hair and pale blue eyes. The news story did not reveal how the Memphis police had obtained even that much information about the killer.

Jim finished reading the article and handed the story to Randy.

"Millicent and this fellow, Kellerman, disappeared from St. Louis as though they'd been wiped from the face of the earth," Edward said. "The constabulary here have no definite idea where they've gone, though Commissioner Bowen thought New Orleans would be as likely a place as any, since Kellerman has some business contacts there."

"If they've left St. Louis," Tommie said, "they reserved their steamer or stagecoach tickets under assumed names."

"Why would they do that?" Jim asked, puzzled.

Edward shrugged. "Your guess is as good as mine," he said. "The only reason that has occurred to me is that Millicent knows I'll come searching for her and is deliberately covering her tracks."

"Perhaps we're wrong to search for her," Jim said. "She's of age, after all, and she's free to do whatever she wishes."

"You wouldn't say that if you'd seen her on board ship coming down the Missouri," Tommie told him. "She behaved as though she was a woman possessed, as though she had little control over what she was doing. True, she helped Edward turn the tables on de Cordova, but the minute Sergeant Kellerman came on the scene to investigate, it was as though she lost all control of herself again."

"That means we can't leave her to her own devices," Edward said, picking up the theme from her. "We feel compelled to find Millicent and, if necessary, to protect her—from herself. At first our intentions were to go directly to New Orleans to find her. Then we saw the story from Memphis in the newspaper. So now we propose to stop off at Memphis and talk with the police authorities there."

Randy Savage was puzzled. "I fail to see the connection," he said, "between the missing Millicent Randall and Karl Kellerman and the deaths of the gangsters in Memphis."

"I'm sorry," Edward said. "I should have made it clear from the start that the description of the possible killer, vague though it is, fits Kellerman almost exactly. We want to give the information to the Memphis police. That news story is also why we asked you to meet us here in St. Louis before we started out."

Randy still looked confused.

"Kellerman is a murderer," Tommie explained. "He has Millicent in his possession. If we're going to apprehend him and rescue Millicent, we're going to need all the help we can get!"

Toby Holt was returning to his ranch from a visit to Portland, going down the trail that followed the course of the Columbia River. The sturdy, sandy-haired twenty-nine-year-old, sinewy and lean as whipcord, breathed deeply, enjoying the scent of pines and incredibly fresh mountain air. Like his late father, Whip Holt, he knew utter contentment on the ranch. He had acquired a national reputation as a surveyor for railroad lines, as an Indian fighter, and as a troubleshooter for presidents of the United States, but he was never happier than when he was at home.

His stallion needed no urging either. The great beast increased his speed as he headed toward home.

A surprise awaited Toby as he neared the cleared pasture lands that surrounded the ranch buildings. From a trail in the pine woods off to his left, there emerged a small figure on the back of a rapidly moving pony, a three-year-old boy in complete western attire, even to his boots and broad-brimmed hat.

"Hello, Papa!" the child called cheerfully.

"Well, hello, Timmy," Toby replied with a grin,

and began to search for his wife. He finally caught a glimpse of her, mounted on her mare, partially concealed in the deep woods, and he realized that the wonderful, ever-sensible Clarissa was allowing the boy to ride ahead of her so that he would feel he had been riding all by himself.

Toby was quick to go along with the game. "Where are you going, Tim?" he asked.

The child pointed in the direction of the ranch house. "We race!" he announced.

"That's a fine idea, son," Toby said gravely. "Let's race! One—two—three—go!" Before he was through counting, Tim, crouched low in the saddle, had started off in the direction of the house, his pony's hooves pounding the hard ground of the trail. Toby deliberately reined in his own mount and allowed his son to beat him by several lengths.

Tim was ecstatic. "I won! I won!" he shouted, and hugged his father as Toby lifted him to the ground.

Clarissa approached, and Tim danced around her as she, too, dismounted. "I raced Papa, and I won, Mama. I beat him!"

Sharing his delight, she bent down, picked him up, and kissed him. "I know you won, Timothy," she said. "I saw you. Congratulations."

They made a handsome family: the tall, statuesque Clarissa in her riding dress, her thick red hair piled up under her broad-brimmed hat; the rugged, lean Toby, who more and more bore a resemblance to his legendary father; and the animated little boy, whose youthful features reflected those of both his parents.

Approaching on foot was Stalking Horse, his face bronzed and deeply lined but his bearing erect and sure. The elderly Cherokee had been foreman of the ranch ever since Whip Holt had founded the place.

Tim hurtled toward the Indian, shouting his news. Stalking Horse listened, made an appropriate comment, and then waved Toby and Clarissa toward the house. "Leave your horses," he called. "Timmy will help me get the saddles off and turn the mounts out to pasture."

Satisfied that their son was in good hands, the couple started toward the house together, their shoulders touching. "That boy is a marvel," Toby said. "When I first saw him, I thought for a split second that he was out riding alone."

"There's no way on earth that I'd let him out of my sight," Clarissa replied. "He's too much like his father."

"I'm not sure if that's an insult or a compliment," Toby told her.

She giggled. "It's a fact," she said. "At the age of three he's already a complete Holt. He's too young to realize that he had a famous grandfather and has an equally famous father, but those things don't matter to him. He's already competing like mad with both of you, and someday, he's going to surpass you. I almost feel sorry for his wife."

Toby's face clouded as they entered the kitchen

and Clarissa poured him a mug of coffee from the pot warming on the stove. "I'm not sure how you mean that," Toby said, "but I'm afraid I take it in the worst way. I apologize to you for all the heartache and inconvenience I've caused you."

She looked up at him, her face registering both alarm and compassion. "Don't be silly, darling," she said.

"We've had some rough times," he insisted.

"But we've overcome them, and that's what counts," Clarissa countered. "Of course we've had hard going from time to time. That's the nature of marriage, but it's what people feel for each other that matters. We love each other, so I can't think of anything that could be better." Saying this, she put her arms around her husband.

As they held each other, Clarissa and Toby sensed that this was a moment of perfect communion. They had no need for further words. They were one in spirit, and their love presented an unbreakable barrier between them and the world.

That night after Tim had been put to bed, Toby and Clarissa were joined at dinner by Stalking Horse and White Elk, a nine-year-old Arapaho orphan who had been jointly adopted by the Cherokee foreman and by Pamela Randall. The boy divided his time between them, and it was their hope that he would grow up to represent the best of both the Indians' and the white man's worlds.

The dinner table was laden with platters of delicious, steaming foods, most of which were produced on the Holt ranch. The roast beef came from the cattle that were raised here, the carrots, peas, onions, and potatoes were grown in Clarissa's large vegetable garden, and the apples and peaches that were used in the pies for this evening's dessert came from the ranch's own fruit trees. Only the flour used in the bread and piecrust came from the market in Portland, but even then, Clarissa baked her own bread and pastries, using the fresh butter that was made from the cream of the ranch's dairy cows.

White Elk was very much at home at a dinner table, handling a knife and fork with ease and taking an intelligent part in the conversation. "The weather grows warmer, and snow is gone from the mountains," he said in fluent English, "but the Arapaho will not go on the warpath this year against their white brothers. I am sure of it."

Stalking Horse exchanged a quick look with Toby and decided the flat statement could not be allowed unchallenged. "What makes White Elk so certain of what will be?" he asked.

The boy looked gravely at the old man. "The government has given the Arapaho new hunting grounds that lie in the north of the territory," White Elk said, "far from the new railroad tracks. We went hunting in that region, and my grandfather will remember that game was plentiful and the rivers were filled with plump fish."

Toby decided to test the boy. "Why should good hunting grounds make a difference?"

White Elk instantly rose to the challenge. "Indians

are like their white brothers," he said. "When their
bellies are full and they have the promise of more
food that is easy to get, they are at peace and will
stay at peace."

"Good boy, White Elk," Clarissa said. "Pass me
your plate so I can give you another slice of roast
beef and some more potatoes. As for you two," she
went on to her husband and Stalking Horse, "leave
the child alone so he can finish his supper in peace."

Toby had sufficient respect for his wife not to
argue the matter. He ate in silence for a time, but
his mind was churning. "Stalking Horse," he said at
last, "when I was in Portland this afternoon, I called
on the chief of police, Peter Thoman, but his office
told me that he's attending a meeting in San Francisco and won't be back until the end of the week. I
reckon I'll have to wait until the beginning of next
week before I have myself deputized."

The elderly Cherokee nodded complacently.
"Plenty of time," he said.

Clarissa kept her own counsel. She knew that
her husband was getting deputized because he had
volunteered to get to the bottom of the vicious attack
on Wong Ke, Toby's wealthy Chinese business men-
tor and friend, who had been mysteriously beaten
while on a recent visit to Portland. Ke and his partner,
Chet Harris—one of the original members of the first
wagon train to Oregon and now a successful business-
man in San Francisco—had indicated that members
of an illegal Chinese criminal gang—or tong—had
been responsible, and Toby was determined to even

the score and teach his elderly friend's attackers a lesson they would not forget.

Glancing at her husband, Clarissa knew it was useless to argue with him. He would be impervious to warnings that it might be dangerous for him to investigate the incident and that it would be best to forget the matter and leave well enough alone. When a Holt's sense of justice was disturbed, he moved heaven and earth until he felt a wrong had been righted, and Clarissa knew it would be a waste of time to speak to Toby about the matter until he had obtained vengeance for Wong Ke.

Toby saw the worry in his wife's eyes and wanted to reassure her, to tell her that everything would work out fine, but in all honesty, he could not. He had a strange premonition that he was in danger. A new incident, in some way connected with the attack on Wong Ke, would take place in the near future, and his life would be threatened by it. But he could not allow that knowledge to deter him from doing what he regarded as his duty, however, just as he could not bring himself to mention the potential danger to Clarissa, worried as she was already.

II

II

Karl Kellerman was tiptoeing out of the hotel suite when Millicent Randall half sat up in the bed and called to him softly.

"Go back to sleep," he said, turning to her. "I've got an important business appointment this morning, so you may as well sleep until noon. I'll come back and pick you up in time for dinner."

Falling back on the pillows, with her thick brown hair framing her face, she raised her arms to him. He came to the bed and bent down to kiss her dutifully, and she threw her arms around his neck and tried to pull him into the bed with her. Lifting her face, she kissed him passionately.

Karl returned her kiss briefly, then managed to extricate himself from her grasp. "Lovemaking will have to wait until later," he told her, speaking softly. "I have a business appointment that I simply must keep."

Millicent sighed petulantly, then dropped her

arms and watched him as he silently let himself out of the suite.

Stopping first for a light breakfast in the hotel's restaurant, Karl then started out on foot across the city. As he drew nearer to the docks on the Mississippi River waterfront, the neighborhood changed from one of wealth to one of penury. The buildings grew shabbier, the clothing and food shops here were inexpensive, and there were a number of cheap brothels. The men and women on the streets were wearing rough, working-class attire, and Karl was conspicuous in his expensive clothes.

When he was about two blocks from the river, he came to a little building on which a small sign was hanging, identifying it as Dugald's Bar. As he entered, Karl saw that the place was crowded with merchant seamen, presumably from a recently arrived freighter, even though the hour was early. Waiting on the customers was a mild-mannered little Scotsman with gray hair, Wallace Dugald, Karl's partner and co-owner of the bar. In spite of his gentleness, Dugald was sufficiently authoritative to keep the unruly customers in line.

Dugald nodded to Karl as he carried a tray of drinks to a table in a far corner. Karl sauntered behind the bar and poured himself a glass of beer. While he was sipping it, Wallace Dugald returned to his post as bartender.

"I read in the papers that you retired from the St. Louis constabulary, Karl. I've been expecting you to show up here any day now. Welcome to New Orleans."

"Thanks, partner," Karl replied jocularly. "It's good to be here. I never spent much time in this place since the day that I provided you with the financing in return for fifty percent, but still it feels like home."

"Just say the word," Dugald told him, "and it'll *be* home. I'm not complaining about our business arrangement, but I'd be delighted to have you working here side by side with me."

"Thanks very much, Wallace," Karl said, "but I'm not sure yet what I'm going to do to earn my living. I spent a lot of years on the police force, so I want to take my time deciding what I'm going to do from here on in. It's a decision that I can't make too quickly."

Wallace looked owlish when he grinned. "As soon as the customers clear out of here," he said, "I've got a surprise for you. Maybe it'll help you make up your mind."

Not understanding the significance of the remark, Karl shrugged and said, "In the meantime, let me give you a hand behind the bar. That'll speed things up a bit." He hung up his jacket, rolled up his shirt-sleeves, and began to pour drinks swiftly and efficiently.

The merchant seamen left the bar late in the morning to search for girls, and Wallace turned to Karl. "We have just enough time for you to see the surprise," he said, "before the noon crowd begins to arrive." He led the way behind the bar to the far end, and there raised a trapdoor in the floor, which revealed a narrow flight of stairs that led to a cellar.

Following him through the trapdoor, Karl descended to the cellar. The only light was provided by a stubby candle that Dugald had lit and now carried in a battered brass holder.

Wallace crossed the room and went to an old-fashioned iron safe, which, after he put down the candle, he opened with a key. Inside were two identical cloth bags that made a clinking sound when he moved them.

"Here," he said, "are the profits from one full year of operations. I had the money changed into gold coins at the bank because they take up less space, and I divided them equally. One of these is yours, and the other is mine. If you like you can go over my accounts for the year, and I'm sure you'll find they'll tally to the penny."

"That won't be necessary," Karl said, and picking up one of the bags, he weighed it experimentally in his hands. His legitimate share of the profits amounted to a good deal of money, but he knew there were still not sufficient funds to pay for keeping up his hotel suite, meals at good eating places, and other expensive habits.

"I don't have to look at the ledgers or count the money, Wallace," he said. "I trust you. After all, we're partners!"

Wallace was pleased. "I'm glad you feel that

way, Karl," he replied. "I've never trusted banks, which is why I've kept the profits right here in the safe. Go on, take your share now."

"I'm in no hurry," Kellerman said. "The gold won't rust in your safe, so I'll leave it right where it is until I decide how to use it."

His mind racing, he already was making cold-blooded plans. Somehow—in a manner yet to be determined—he would dispose of Wallace Dugald permanently. Then he would take both bags of gold. The combined profits would provide him with a nest egg sufficient to live in the manner to which he was growing accustomed. Adding to this the money he would earn doing the job involving the crime boss Domino, he would have a small fortune. He would be able to afford the company of the blonde on whom he had an eye, and Millicent Randall be damned!

Suddenly the whole future looked bright. "It sure was a lucky day," he said, "when you and I became partners."

Millicent, wearing an expensive, revealing gown, dined with Karl at one of New Orleans's fanciest restaurants. She was supremely happy. The food and wines were perfect, every patron in the place took notice of her, and her lover was strong, handsome, and impressively virile. She was prepared for a wonderful evening and was stunned when Karl said to her, "I'll drop you off at the hotel after dinner. I have some business that requires my attention this evening."

"You left me to go on business this morning, too," she said indignantly.

"I've got to work," he said.

She couldn't help pouting. "At this time of night?"

"Night, day, any time at all," he replied, his manner brutal. "The money doesn't grow on trees to pay for supper at a place like this, and I don't find the cash in the streets to buy you dresses like you're wearing tonight."

"I—I'm sorry, Karl," she murmured. "I don't mean to be a burden on you."

"You're no burden," he told her, "but I've got to have the freedom to do what I must to earn a living for us."

"I'm ready to go back to the hotel," she said meekly. "Try not to be too late tonight."

He replied coldly, "I have no idea what time I'll be coming back tonight. Don't wait up for me."

Karl walked Millicent back to their hotel and then continued on his way, going rapidly to Dugald's Bar. There he changed into the inconspicuous attire of a working man: flannel shirt and woolen trousers. Dugald, meanwhile, was busy serving customers.

Karl stood for a time at the rear of the establishment inspecting the patrons; finally he settled on a grizzled man who sat alone at a table. The tarnished gold braid on his cap and on his cuffs revealed that he was a merchant marine captain. The officer interested Karl, and he decided this might be the kind of man he was looking for.

After pouring himself a tankard of ale and picking up a bottle of whiskey, Karl took the empty seat across from the captain. They soon fell into conversation, and Karl encouraged the relationship by pouring the officer a fresh drink from time to time.

The man, seemingly mild-mannered and quiet, was Captain Robin Kayross, a Greek sea captain. He was the master of a large steam-propelled freighter, the *Diana*, which plied the seas between New Orleans and Hong Kong. It developed that he was not self-employed but was hired by the ship's owners, who lived in San Francisco.

After several of the strong drinks that Karl quietly poured for him, Captain Kayross began to discuss his lot in life more freely. "There are some," he said, "who envy me. They think that being master of my own ship must be paradise. Well, it isn't. I don't mind telling you that except for a few fellow Greeks—some of my officers and about half a dozen members of my crew—I have hell's own time keeping a full crew. Every chance they get—and in almost every port I visit—officers and crew jump ship, and I've got to begin again the whole process of recruiting. It gets harder and harder."

"Is there any particular reason they jump ship?" Karl asked with pretended innocence.

Robin Kayross snorted. "They have fifty reasons," he said stridently. "For one thing, they complain day and night about the quality of the food I serve. I'll admit the diet is monotonous because I save money by buying foods in large quantities, but nobody ever gets sick and dies from what he eats on board the *Diana*. If I can tolerate the meals, so can my crew!"

Karl wore his most interested-looking expression as he poured out another drink for the captain.

Kayross continued, "No matter how many men I sign on, they always claim that the crew is short-handed. It doesn't matter if I put to sea with twenty men or with thirty, I hear the same thing. Well, sir, I don't mind telling you that I don't believe in coddling sailors. When a man goes to work for me, he can expect to work long, hard hours for his money. Putting to sea on the *Diana* is no vacation, and every last man who works for me finds that out in a hurry. Either he works or he feels the bite of a rope's end on his bare back, and there's no two ways about it. So I'm less than popular with my crew, particularly as I hold back pay as an incentive for working hard. They claim that often I withhold their wages completely, but I'm damned if they can ever prove it."

The man was totally lacking in scruples, Karl thought, and that was all to the good.

"I'm not saying I'm all that unhappy," the captain went on, chuckling quietly. "One way or another I manage to fill my purse, and that's what really counts. What my crews don't know won't hurt them, and the same thing goes for the ship's owners. All the same, hiring conditions are so bad that I swear to you in the name of Beelzebub that I'd give almost anything to have a crew made up of shang-haied seamen. That way there'd be no problem. They'd work their tails off or get whipped for their pains. They'd get fed whatever slops we wanted to give them and would be damn glad to get them. They'd get a few hours of rest at night, just enough to keep them going all the next day, and I wouldn't hear a peep out of them. There's only one way to run a ship! With whips and chains!"

Karl sipped his own drink and stared thought-fully into the contents of his glass. "I wish I knew whether you were serious or joking," he said softly. "I could make suggestions about how to go about shanghaiing some men if you were really serious."

Kayross was suddenly cautious. "How do I know you're not a member of the New Orleans constabulary?" he demanded. "How do I know you aren't assigned to a squad that's trying to break up the gangs that are impressing ordinary citizens as seamen?"

"I tell you plain, and I tell you true, that I don't represent any constabulary," Karl said emphatically. "I have no power to arrest anyone. You can believe me or not, as you choose, and if you get it into your head that I'm trying to trick you, then be damned to you!"

"It does no harm," Kayross said, "to be careful."

"No harm at all," Karl replied. "To show you *I* meant no harm, have another bottle—on me."

"I'll have another if you'll drink with me." Kayross had no intention of getting drunk while this burly stranger remained sober.

Karl went behind the bar and took a bottle. "You and your Greeks," he said, returning to the table and pouring out two whiskeys, "could try to kidnap yourselves a crew off the streets of New Orleans, though to be sure, gathering a full complement of men by impressment can be a very dangerous pastime."

"Especially in a foreign country where you have no friends on the bench," the Greek said. "That's why I'd much rather pay cash for merchandise. It's safer and neater."

Karl sipped his drink, then stared at the sea captain over the rim of his glass. "Let me get this straight," he said. "You're willing to put up a certain amount of money in cash for every shanghaied seaman who's handed over to you. Is that correct?"

Kayross examined the contents of his drink and then raised his glass to his lips. "You have the general idea," he said.

Kellerman had grown tired of fencing. "How much?" he demanded brusquely.

The captain was reluctant to name a figure, but his hand was being forced. "I'll pay five hundred dollars," he said, "for every man who's handed over to me, free and clear, to work on board the *Diana*."

The former St. Louis detective laughed as though really enjoying himself. "Suppose I made a deal with you," he said. "I'd be taking all the risks, and I sure wouldn't lift a finger for a rotten five hundred dollars a head. It just wouldn't be worth my neck."

"How much would you want?" Kayross demanded.

"One thousand dollars per man."

"A thousand dollars!" Kayross acted as though he had been stabbed. "I don't operate a freighter in the rich Atlantic service, you know. I'm forced to take the long route around South America to the Orient, where I'm subject to the bargaining wiles of the Chinese. All I can afford to pay is seven hundred dollars per man and not one cent more."

Kellerman shook his head sadly. "All you have to do," he said, "is rustle up cash for your payments, but I've got to take chances with every man I impress. I can't go any lower than a rock-bottom fee of eight hundred dollars per shanghaied man. Take it or leave it."

Seemingly lost in thought, Kayross stared at the contents of his glass. Then he helped himself to a small sip, smiled bleakly, and said, "You have a deal."

They shook hands, and at Kellerman's suggestion they adjourned to the waterfront in order to inspect the *Diana*. They walked together to the docks and soon came to the steam-powered ship. She was about fifteen years old and had been subjected to careless treatment. Litter was scattered on her decks, and she was badly in need of paint.

As Kellerman accompanied the captain on board, however, he noted with approval that the Greek seamen on duty were carrying loaded rifles.

Captain Kayross led his visitor below to the

hold, the boiler room, and the coal storage quarters, where the shanghaied seamen would be chained until the *Diana* was far out at sea. Cockroaches were everywhere underfoot, and an insistent series of scratching sounds indicated that numerous rats were scurrying out of the path of the approaching humans. None of that mattered to Karl. All he could think of was the money he would make providing a crew for this disreputable ship.

Cindy Holt, the pretty, vivacious twenty-year-old daughter of the famous Whip Holt and stepdaughter of Major General Leland Blake, commander of the U.S. Army in the West, was home at Fort Vancouver, Washington, from Oregon State College for the summer holidays. Her mother and stepfather had been called away on a military inspection trip, so she eagerly accepted the written invitation awaiting her from her sister-in-law, Clarissa. It was always a treat to eat supper and stay overnight at the ranch house, visiting with her brother Toby and with Clarissa and little Tim. She needed only the presence of her fiancé, Cadet Henry Blake of the U.S. Military Academy, the adopted son of her mother and General Blake, to complete her joy. She and Hank, a high honors student at West Point, had a private understanding, and she comforted herself with the thought that in two more years, after he won his commission as an army officer, they would be able to marry. Until then, she was learning to exercise patience.

General Blake's boat carried Cindy and her mare across the Columbia River to Oregon, and avoiding the town of Portland, where she intended to visit friends later during her stay, Cindy struck out at once for the Holt ranch.

The summer air was warm and fragrant, and a long, lovely twilight softened the mountains in the background. Cindy's mare, thoroughly enjoying the occasion, too, began to canter of her own volition.

All at once, Cindy saw a sight that made her blood run cold. Stretched out stiff-legged in the underbrush off to the left ahead of her was a gelding that had been shot and killed. On the opposite side of the trail, a man lay stretched on the ground, and his shirt, soaked and caked with blood, indicated that he, too, had been shot.

The man opened his eyes with a great effort and managed to focus on the young woman as she approached him and dismounted.

Slowly and with great deliberation, he began to fumble with his belt. "He searched me," he muttered hoarsely, "after he shot me, but I had the papers hidden in . . . secret compartment. Please see that they reach . . . General Blake. Tell him that government courier did his best." With a hand that trembled, he gave the girl several sheets of very thin paper that were folded into a small square.

Cindy took the folded papers from him, not bothering to explain that she was General Blake's stepdaughter. She knew the man had been wounded too badly for her to help him unaided, and she bent over him, intending to ask him what she could do for him before she went to her brother's ranch for help. But she realized with dismay that the man had stopped breathing and had already died.

As Cindy, now deeply upset, rose to her feet, dropping the papers she had been given into the pocket of the buckskin jacket she wore, she sensed rather than saw that someone was lurking nearby.

Suddenly a shot rang out, and a bullet whistled near her.

Truly the daughter of Whip Holt, Cindy reacted coolly. She snatched her own rifle from the saddle sling, raised it to her shoulder as she wheeled, and fired in the direction from which the bullet had come. Thrashing sounds in the underbrush told her she might not have missed her mark by much.

Taking advantage of the brief respite, she leaped into the saddle, dug her heels into the mare's flanks, and was off to a flying start in the direction of the Holt ranch. She bent low in the saddle as two shots rang out and a pair of bullets passed overhead. One of them was too close for comfort, so she squirmed around in her saddle as her mare continued to plunge forward and sent another shot from her rifle in the direction of her pursuer. When she saw Toby's ranch house and the outbuildings directly ahead, she knew that she was out of the range of her enemy.

Toby had heard the sounds of gunfire and had come into the open carrying his own rifle. Now he saw his sister riding toward him at breakneck speed, crouching low in her saddle. As she dismounted she breathlessly told him about the dead messenger and the person who had fired at her.

Stalking Horse and a half-dozen ranch hands now arrived at the scene, and Toby instantly waved them into action. They plunged into the woods, but when Stalking Horse reappeared after about a quarter of an hour, he shook his head. "Nobody is in the woods," he said. "Whoever followed Miss Cindy ran away. That's good for him, because if I find him, I put a bullet into his heart."

Meanwhile, the ranch hands had brought back the body of the messenger, and Toby told two of the hands to take the dead man to the Portland city morgue. Then he led his sister into the house. There, Clarissa awaited them and produced a pot of tea that helped to soothe Cindy, who then repeated her story more calmly.

Toby unfolded the sheets of paper and began to read them. "These are very interesting," he said. "They've been sent by General Layton at the Presidio in San Francisco, who received them from an anonymous source. They implicate a number of Chinese in San Francisco and several others in Portland in a Chinese smuggling ring."

"What are they smuggling?" Clarissa asked.

"Chinese immigrants principally, in defiance of United States immigration laws, and also opium."

"There are no laws to prevent the importation of opium into the country, are there?" Cindy asked.

Her brother shook his head. "No, but there's a strong ground swell of public opinion against the importation of opium. A large number of upstanding citizens claim that when it's used for nonmedical purposes, it's extremely harmful. It seems that members of a San Francisco tong have been making a vast sum of money on opium and immigration."

"Do you suppose," Clarissa asked thoughtfully, "that there's any connection between the tong that's involved in this smuggling operation and the attack on Wong Ke?"

"Perhaps," he replied, "though since the source is anonymous, there's no way to press any charges. General Layton was sending the papers to General Blake for his opinion. In any event, I promised Ke and Chet that I'd look into the involvements of the tong carefully, and this is the first lead of any kind that we've been given."

"One thing is for certain," Cindy said. "Someone is going to great lengths to prevent the authorities from learning too much. The courier carrying this information was murdered, and whoever killed him sure did try to stop me from leaving the scene of the killing with the papers."

Toby nodded thoughtfully, then said, "With the general out of town, I'll do the next best thing and take these documents to Peter Thoman, the Portland police chief, and to Tilman Wade, the director of security for the state. They're back in town now and may know something more."

They dropped the subject and devoted the rest of the evening to family matters. Little Tim had not yet retired, so his aunt sat with him while he ate his supper and then she told him a bedtime story. Later, at the dinner table, the talk centered on Cindy's recent activities and the news that she heard from Hank Blake in her correspondence with him.

After breakfast the following morning, Toby saddled his stallion and started into Portland carrying the courier's documents. He was satisfied that, in the absence of General Blake, the interests of the public were well served. Chief Peter Thoman was the son of Paul Thoman, one of the original settlers, and ably represented the younger generation. Tough old Tilman Wade, the state director of security, had also traveled to Oregon on the first wagon train to cross the continent, and he was unyielding in his fight against criminals. Together the combination of youth and age formed a team that had enjoyed remarkable success in its fight against crime. Oregon ranked high among the states in its record of protecting its citizens from criminal elements.

As Toby rode quietly through the pine woods, banks of clouds appeared overhead. Glancing up at the sky, he knew that rain would fall later in the day.

Suddenly the explosive crash of a rifle shot shattered the morning silence, and a bullet whined past Toby's head.

Reacting immediately, he urged his stallion to a full gallop in the direction of where the shot had come from and grabbed one of his pistols. Crouching low in the saddle, he was prepared to shoot as soon as he caught a glimpse of the man who had fired at him.

No more than a half minute elapsed before Toby caught a glimpse of another rider far ahead in the woods, beating a hasty retreat from the scene. Still riding hard, Toby aimed his pistol and fired a shot at the fleeing figure. The distance was too great, however, and the rider disappeared from sight into the thick pine woods that extended for a considerable distance in all directions before finally giving way to cleared land on the approach to Portland. The rider could enter the city at any one of a score of places, and his tracks would be lost among those of the hundreds of other horses and vehicles in the area. Further pursuit would be a waste of time, and Toby reholstered his pistol regretfully, realizing that his would-be killer was free to renew his assault at some later date.

Toby continued on his way toward the city. Obviously he had been shot at because he was suspected of carrying the papers that had resulted in the death of the courier. Someone was very anxious that these documents be intercepted and not passed on to the authorities.

The courthouse on Fourth Street was a large, imposing building, like the other public structures located on one of two adjacent parklike public squares. Here were the offices of federal, state, and local officials. The second-floor office of Tilman Wade over-looked bustling Fourth Street, and Toby stood with the balding Wade while they awaited the arrival of Chief Thoman.

"If your pa was still alive," the older man said, "he'd be every bit as amazed as I am. There was nothing but trees and bare land here when we finally called a halt to our wagon train, and today the population of Portland is about eight thousand people. What really astonishes me is the prediction that we'll have double that number by the time 1880 comes. The faster the town grows, the more complicated the job of maintaining public order becomes."

"I don't envy you, Tilman. It was a lot simpler in my father's day when he and a half-dozen others kept the peace by keeping their rifles oiled."

They were interrupted by the arrival of Peter Thoman, who was exceptionally tall, extremely thin, and was acknowledged to be a very efficient police chief.

Toby told the officials his sister's experience the previous evening, then showed them the documents she had been given by the dying courier. He also told them of the attempt on his own life less than an hour earlier.

Both men read the papers with interest. "You will note," the police chief said, "that the tong is never mentioned by name. That's because no out-sider ever learns its name. That is one of the secrets the Chinese guard zealously. However, there is no doubt in my mind who the head of this tong now is. Kung Lee is his name, and he has effectively elimi- nated the former leaders and has seized complete control, showing no mercy to them or to anyone else. If my memory serves correctly, Wong Ke told you that Kung was responsible for the attack on him."

Tilman Wade fingered the butts of the Colt repeating pistols that he carried in his belt. "Even without these papers," he said, "I'd be inclined to suspect a tong headed by Kung. They've demon- strated repeatedly that they have no respect for Ameri- can laws. They're a vicious group."

"Well, we agreed that I was going to be depu- tized as a federal marshal so that I could go after the tong," Toby said matter-of-factly. "I guess now is as good a time as any."

Tilman looked very much concerned. "The cir- cuit judge is sitting in the federal court, all ready to swear you in, Toby," he said, "but are you really sure you want to take on the responsibility for chas- ing after Kung Lee's gang? I mean, here you've finally gained the chance to settle with your family on your ranch and to live like an ordinary citizen."

"I promised Wong Ke and Chet Harris that I'd do all I could to track down the ruffians who attacked Ke," Toby said solemnly, "and I'm going to keep my word to them. They're not only business associates; they're like family to me, and I'm very much in their debt. In addition to which, I don't like the idea of the tong defrauding the American public by illegally importing Chinese laborers and bringing large amounts of opium into this country. It's my duty as a citizen to help put a stop to such practices."

"You've more than earned your share of good citizenship, Toby," Peter Thoman said. "This country would be in great shape if everybody's contribution equaled yours."

Karl Kellerman claimed that business affairs would keep him occupied all day, so Millicent was once again thrown on her own resources. Dressing modestly and with just a trace of makeup, she spent a couple of hours shopping and then returned to the Louisiana House for a noon dinner, sitting alone on the far side of the dining room as the orchestra played classical selections.

Before she had a chance to study the menu, the hotel manager appeared at her elbow. "Madame Kellerman," he said, using the name under which she was registered, "may I have the honor of presenting to you Mr. Jean-Pierre Gautier, a member of a prominent New Orleans family, who also happens to be a majority stockholder in this hotel."

Millicent looked up at the thin, extremely well-dressed, dark-haired young man who was bowing to the waist before her. He was the one who had shadowed her whenever she had been alone, following her into shops and restaurants and keeping watch over her on the streets. She pretended, however, never to have seen him before and simply extended her hand and murmured, "How do you do."

He handled her fingers as though they were made of the most fragile glass. "I am overwhelmed, Madame Kellerman," he said. "If you are not expecting anyone for dinner, may I join you?"

His sincerity was so obvious that she was amused as well as flattered, despite her earlier resolve to avoid him at all costs. What was more, Karl seemed not to care what she did, and so she told him, "Sit down, by all means."

He promptly took the chair opposite her and asked for the privilege of buying her an aperitif. She consented graciously, and he immediately ordered from the hotel manager, who went off to get a waiter to serve them.

"I hope," he said, "that you don't mind the presence of the orchestra. They're one of the additions to the hotel for which I'm responsible."

She laughed aloud. "How could I not like the music of Brahms," she said, "especially the waltzes?"

He was impressed. "You are a musician, Madame Kellerman?"

"My name isn't Kellerman," she said. "I'm Millicent Randall, the name I had when I was born, and I am indeed a musician. I play the flute, and I studied for many years at the Baltimore Conservatory, where I also composed for the flute."

"I'd love to hear your compositions," he said. "I'm afraid I have no musical talents myself, although

I much appreciate music. The most I can claim is that I do my part in sponsoring the symphony orchestra here." They had quickly discovered a mutual interest in music and discussed nothing else as they each drank two glasses of wine. Millicent had not had the opportunity to talk about music with anyone since she had left Baltimore, and she chatted happily, feeling as though floodgates had been unexpectedly opened in her.

In time, Jean-Pierre revealed his own background. He was the heir to one of the larger French fortunes in New Orleans and had been married to a woman whom he had loved dearly and who had died after a long and painful illness the year before. He made no secret of the fact that he had been captured by the very sight of Millicent, and ever since she had come to town some days earlier, he had spent most of his waking hours trying to arrange an introduction to her.

She was somewhat less than frank in her response to him. She spoke freely of her life in Baltimore and subsequently of her travels in the West and the establishment of her cousin's ranch in Idaho, but she offered no explanation whatever of how she happened to come to New Orleans, and she blithely ignored the existence of Karl Kellerman.

When Jean-Pierre asked for the privilege of seeing her again, she became equally elusive, telling him she would be happy to meet him for a noon or evening dinner but that it was impossible for her to set up engagements far in advance. What she did not tell him was that her day-to-day existence was still ruled by Kellerman's whims. When he had business that took him elsewhere, she was forgotten. But when he wanted her company, he expected her to be immediately available to him.

Jean-Pierre, however, seemed more than satisfied with any arrangements she cared to make, even though her planning was tenuous at best.

By the time they finished dinner, parting company when they left the table, it was obvious that Jean-Pierre Gautier was infatuated with her. Millicent was relieved, even though she knew it was selfish to feel as she did. The fear had been growing within her for several days that Karl might desert her, and she wondered what she would do if she found herself alone in a strange city. Jean-Pierre offered her a measure of security, however, and she was grateful that she had met him. In spite of her outward sophistication, she was afraid to face the world alone, and she felt better able to cope knowing that Jean-Pierre was ready and able to assist her in every way possible.

Occupying the ground floor of the dilapidated wooden building in San Francisco's Chinatown was a curio shop that sold trinkets and souvenirs of China. On the second floor, at the far end of a rickety wooden staircase, were quarters that casual visitors to the shop assumed to be the home of the proprietors of the modest little establishment. But beyond a door of heavy oak, a surprise awaited the few persons ever to gain admission to the place. Here, the floors were covered with magnificent, handwoven Oriental rugs. On them stood superbly wrought vases and statuettes of porcelain, and on the walls hung precious Chinese paintings. At a glance, the place represented the Orient at its most sumptuous. A room on one side of the suite was furnished like an American office, however. Here stood a large, mahogany desk, a reclining chair, and a number of visitors' chairs of carved oak. The walls were graced with expensive portraits by American artists.

Behind the huge desk sat Kung Lee, the tong leader who was said to be the most powerful Chinese man in North America. In his mandarin robes of black he did not look like a man of power, however. His build was frail, his hair was gray, and he wore horn-rimmed glasses. He could have been anywhere from fifty to seventy-five years old. His right hand moving delicately, swiftly, he was writing a letter, his brush strokes firm as he made the Chinese characters.

His efforts were interrupted when a nondescript-looking serving man in black jacket and trousers came into the room and bowed. "Forgive the intrusion, Celestial Leader," he said, speaking in the educated Mandarin tongue, "but Chung Ai has just returned to San Francisco from Portland and craves an audience with you."

Kung Lee sighed, slightly annoyed by the interruption. "Send Ho Tai to me," he said, "and after he has entered this room, wait for a few moments, then show in Chung Ai."

Ho Tai, a burly native of the north of China, ambled into the room. His appearance was unlike that of the scholarly Kung Lee in every way. The newcomer was short and squat, a man with a knife-scarred face. He carried a double-edged blade of exceptional sharpness in the belt of his all-black attire.

Ho Tai bowed to Kung Lee, but there was no conversation between them. The older man's gaze rested on his henchman for a moment, and Ho Tai seemed to know what was expected of him. He moved silently to a corner of the room, his step surprisingly graceful for someone of his build, and there he folded his arms and stared impassively straight ahead.

The door opened again, and Chung Ai advanced noiselessly into the room. He bowed low before Kung Lee, who offered him a chair, which he sank into gracefully, ignoring the presence of Ho Tai. Chung Ai was dressed like a ranch hand in an open-throated flannel shirt and worn work pants stuffed into calf-high boots. He wore a brace of pistols in his belt, and in one hand he carried a broad-brimmed hat.

Chung Ai reported diligently and at length on his most recent activities. He related how he had shot the horse of the official U.S. courier and, after bringing down the animal, had proceeded to put another bullet into the man. Before the courier had died, Chung Ai had searched him in vain for the precious documents that he was taking to General Blake at U.S. Army headquarters. He had been diverted from his task by the arrival of Cindy Holt on the scene and had seen the dying man take the papers from a secret compartment in his belt and give them to her.

Carrying the telltale documents, the girl had escaped and gone to the house of her brother, the famous Toby Holt. The following morning, Holt had started in the direction of Portland when Chung Ai had intercepted him in the forest and had fired at him.

"Ah." Kung Lee pressed his fingertips together and sighed gently.

"With deep regret," Chung Ai said, "I must inform Your Excellency that my attempt to kill Toby Holt failed, and I only just got away with my life. I did not dare to linger and exchange gunfire with Toby Holt. All who have attempted to exchange fire with him in this way have paid for their foolishness with their lives. I would have gained nothing had I engaged in such an exercise."

The older man pursed his lips. "What became of Holt after you shot at him and missed?" he asked.

"He went into Portland, where he met with the authorities. This article appeared in the Portland newspaper." He took a frayed clipping from his shirt pocket and passed it across the desk.

Kung Lee's face remained expressionless as he

read that Toby Holt had been sworn in as a United States deputy marshal.

"I am sure that—at the very least—we can expect interference at some future date from Mr. Holt," Kung Lee said with regret. "I do not look forward to the prospect of such a man as that one meddling in my affairs."

"I offer you a thousand apologies," Chung Ai said. "I did the best I could."

Kung Lee pressed his fingertips together and pronounced sentence. "Failure," he said, "is intolerable to me. I recognize only success. And there has been none. First, you failed to do away with the meddler Wong Ke. Then you failed to stop the courier with the telltale documents. Last, and most grievous, you failed to do away with Toby Holt, who now will become our greatest enemy."

Chung Ai began to explain his position further, but he was so terrified he could only babble.

Kung Lee glanced at Ho Tai, who had remained immobile throughout the conversation. The tong leader inclined his head almost imperceptibly.

Ho Tai moved forward swiftly, his wicked knife glistening in his hand. He struck with lightning speed and cut Chung Ai's throat from ear to ear. Then, just as swiftly, he lifted the dead man's body into his arms before too much blood spilled onto the fine Persian carpet, and took the body out the back door and down the outside stairway. There, in the concealed backyard of the little building, Ho Tai placed the body in a crate labeled *Imported Porcelain* and covered the remains with sawdust. The crate would be sent to a curio shop owned by a rival tong, and the surprised owners would see how Kung Lee dealt with people who failed him.

Meanwhile, Kung Lee sat behind his desk, his eyes rooted to the spot where blood had stained his priceless antique rug. At last he pressed the bell to summon his manservant, and when the man entered and bowed, the tong leader instructed him, "Remove the carpet at once. I'm afraid it has suffered irreparable harm. Fortunately, I have several others that I like equally as well. Put a new carpet in its place, and be sure your hands are clean so you do not soil it!"

III

The police commissioner of Memphis, Charles O'Shea, leaned back in his swivel chair and looked at each of his guests in turn. Edward Blackstone, his handsome face reflecting the seriousness of his intent, anxiously regarded the commissioner, awaiting his statement. Pretty and vivacious Tommie Harding regarded her fiancé—she was far more concerned about his reaction than anything that the head of the Memphis police force might have to say.

"I'm glad," O'Shea said, "that my department isn't alone in showing an interest in the activities of Karl Kellerman. He was a good enough detective during the years that he was on the St. Louis force, but in all my dealings with him, I never trusted him completely. Although I can't put my finger on what was wrong with him, I'm willing to swear that he was less than honest."

"You have no hard evidence, then, that proves

61

his connection with the criminal world?" Edward
asked.

The commissioner shook his head. "We don't
have a shred of it," he replied. "Some of my men go
along with what you think and are prepared to swear
that Kellerman had a hand—quite possibly the major
hand—in the death of the Memphis gang leader and
one of his bodyguards recently. But they can't prove
it, and neither can you. I'd love to get my hands on
him and have a little heart-to-heart chat with him,
but he's too clever, and I'm sure he has his alibis
already worked out."

"Nevertheless, you have no objection if I attempt to speak with him about a certain lady who
was last seen in his company and who happens to be
my cousin?" Edward persisted.

"Not at all," Commissioner O'Shea replied, "and
I have a little information that will be of help to
you." He opened a desk drawer and took out a file.
"I heard from New Orleans just the day before
yesterday. According to the New Orleans police,
Kellerman has indeed turned up there, as you and
Commissioner Bowen in St. Louis surmised. Kellerman is a part owner of a saloon known as Dugald's
Bar in a working-class district, and he's been spending a great deal of time there ever since he got into
town."

"Did the report confirm," Edward asked anxiously, "whether he was traveling with a lady?"

The commissioner studied the report for a few
seconds more and then closed it decisively. "Keller-

man's weakness," he said, "has always been women. He appears to be incapable of leaving them alone. To answer your question more directly, several members of my department saw him when he stayed overnight here, and they said he was traveling with a brown-haired strumpet, if you'll pardon my language, ma'am," he added to Tommie. "Apparently she had the manners of a lady, more so than most of the other women who've associated with him, but in her dress and in the way she made up, she was nothing but a strumpet, plain and simple."

"Unfortunately, Edward," Tommie said softly, "that sounds like an accurate description of Millicent."

"However," the Memphis police commissioner went on, "the report from the New Orleans police doesn't indicate whether this same brunette is still with Kellerman."

Edward did his best to conceal his disappointment. "At the very least," he said, "once we catch up with Kellerman, he'll have to tell us what's become of Millicent. If she isn't with him, at least he should know where she's gone."

"I wish you good luck in tracking down Kellerman," the commissioner said, "and if you don't mind, I'll give you a word of advice: When he wants, Kellerman literally breathes charm, but in his natural state, he's inclined to be ruthless, rough, and very tough."

"We're prepared for all contingencies," Edward said. "I have two strong men in my party who will come to my assistance if there is any trouble. But I also believe that the more informal our get-together, the better it will be, and so I intend first to visit him alone. In the event that Millicent isn't with him, he'll be far more inclined to talk and reveal her whereabouts if he feels that I'm just paying him a quiet, friendly visit."

He and Tommie took their leave of the commissioner soon thereafter, and when they returned to their hotel, they reported on their meeting to Jim Randall and Randy Savage.

"Obviously," Jim said, "we have no real choice in the matter. We'll have to go on to New Orleans, find Kellerman, and ask him for Millicent's whereabouts. At least the end appears to be in sight."

Edward was less certain, after suffering many disappointments, that they would find Millicent soon, but he said nothing about it to the others.

A howling gale blew in from the Gulf of Mexico, and New Orleans was inundated with heavy, steady rains. The weather was perfect for Karl Kellerman's purposes. At his own suggestion, he relieved Wallace Dugald behind the bar of their establishment so that the Scotsman could take a nap. During the next two hours, three solitary drinkers managed to brave the elements and to patronize the bar. Karl accorded each of them the same treatment, putting a drug into their drinks that rendered them unconscious. Then he carried them, one by one, down to the cellar, where he bound them hand and foot and gagged them. He told himself that in return for this minor effort, he had earned twenty-four hundred dollars.

He congratulated himself, reflecting that his timing was perfect. Captain Robin Kayross had promised to come by later that night with several members of his loyal cadre. Karl would be awaiting them, as arranged, with the first of his shanghaied seamen.

Wallace returned from his house after an absence of a little more than two hours, and now Karl intended to put into effect the second part of his plan.

By including Dugald in the ranks of the unfortunates who would be compelled to work their way across the Pacific and back on board the *Diana*, Karl would be able to take complete possession of both bags of gold that reposed in the cellar safe, and any future profits that the bar earned would be exclusively his. In addition, before this night ended, he would perform the gaming house robbery that Domino had set up for him. He would earn large sums before dawn.

As Wallace stood in the entrance, removing his outer clothing, rainwater dripped from him and formed a puddle on the floor of the saloon. "It's pretty fierce out there tonight," he said. "This is the worst weather I've seen in a long time."

"It strikes me this is a good night for us to celebrate," Karl told him.

The very idea struck Wallace as absurd. "What is there to celebrate?"

"We're celebrating the fact that I've joined you here and intend to take an active part in the business."

Wallace became more enthusiastic. "That's great, if you mean it, Karl," he said. "I've been working seven days and seven nights a week, and I can stand some relief now and again."

Karl nodded. "You've been spending far too much time at the bar. It's only common sense that you take it easy, maybe even go on a little trip." His smile broadened as he thought that Wallace would indeed go on a trip very soon.

Sending Wallace to sea as a shanghai victim was by far the best solution to the problem of what to do with him. As a matter of principle, Karl disliked the idea of killing the man responsible for his acquisition of two bags of gold; in addition, if he murdered Wallace, he would have the problem of disposing of his body. Shanghaiing him and sending him to work on board the *Diana* would get rid of him without a trace, and yet Karl's own hands would be clean.

Walking behind the bar he asked, "What will you have?"

Wallace hesitated. "I've always made it a rule never to drink on a night when I'm going to be serving customers."

Karl laughed jovially. "As you can see, there isn't a customer in sight, and judging from the downpour out there, we're going to have the whole evening to ourselves. If I remember correctly, you like rye whiskey and water."

"Right," Wallace replied, beginning to relax. "Make it a mild drink, if you will."

"You bet," Karl told him, busying himself behind the bar. Turning his back to his partner for a few moments in order to conceal what he was doing, he poured into Dugald's drink several drops of the powerful drug that he had purchased at an apothecary shop earlier in the day, the same medicine that had already proved itself with the men who were sleeping in the cellar, bound hand and foot. Satisfied that the medication had no taste and no smell, he handed Wallace the glass, then poured himself a somewhat stronger drink.

"Here's to our partnership," he said. "Long may it continue to flourish." He raised his glass to his lips.

Dugald also drank. "Amen to that," he said, then sipped again. "This tastes pretty good," he went on. "I was colder than I realized. This is really one hell of a rotten night."

For the next quarter of an hour, Karl kept up a light stream of conversation. Afraid that the drug was having no effect, he considered feeding Wallace another dose, but at last his patience was rewarded, and he saw Dugald's eyelids beginning to droop.

"This is very strange," Wallace said thickly. "My drink must be more potent than I realize. I can hardly hold up my head."

Karl thought it best not to reply and waited for the Scotsman to lose consciousness.

Wallace peered at him, eyelids drooping. "This

is strange," he muttered. "You look like you're
gloating, Karl. Why are you gloating?"

Karl still thought it best to make no reply.

"You're up to something!" Wallace cried, his
voice thickening as the drug continued to take effect.
"One mild rye and water wouldn't make me feel like
this. You doped me. You put something in my drink!"

Karl continued to say nothing.

With a last burst of energy, Wallace shook a fist
under the younger man's nose. "I don't know why
you did it, but you've tricked me, Kellerman!" he
cried. "Why have you done this to me? Damn your
soul to hell!"

All at once, he lost consciousness and sagged to
the floor.

Karl's leering grin broadened. He opened the
trapdoor, and throwing his partner over one shoulder,
he descended to the cellar. There he made Dugald's
wrists and ankles secure with lengths of rope, and as
he had done with the other victims, he tied a gag
around his partner's mouth. If he awakened prematurely, he would be unable to make a fuss or call
for help.

Placing the unconscious body next to that of his
other victims, Karl allowed himself a sigh of relief.
For all practical purposes, Wallace Dugald was already confined to the hold of the merchant ship.
Now glancing at his pocket watch, Karl noted that it
was time to leave for the gaming establishment. If he
could keep to his schedule, he would return to the

bar in time to turn over the unconscious men to Captain Kayross.

He left the cellar and felt supremely confident as he slipped a six-shooter into one pocket and a blackjack, a length of lead pipe covered with leather, into another. Donning his hat and coat, he locked up the bar and ignored the elements as he walked briskly to 321 Jefferson.

"I'm here for some action!" he told the guard on duty at the entrance, and pushed his way into the old mansion.

Pausing at a landing on the way to the second floor, Karl tied a bandanna around his face, knotting it at the back of his neck. Then, one hand on the butt of his pistol, he entered the principal game room, shutting the door behind him. There were two card games in progress, and several people were sitting at a bar over which a bartender presided. There were twenty-five to thirty well-dressed patrons in the room, including one man in plain civilian clothes sitting at the bar, whom Karl recognized from meetings he had attended as a lieutenant of New Orleans police. It was obvious that the official was working as a security officer in the place, probably earning a large sum for his after-hours work. But having spotted him in advance, Karl was way ahead of the game; he knew the man could be disarmed before he posed any threat.

Scanning the patrons quickly, Karl was relieved when he saw that Domino was very much engrossed in a game with one of the card dealers. So far, the former detective-sergeant from St. Louis thought, everything was going his way.

"Ladies and gentlemen, give me your attention," Karl called as he took his pistol from his pocket. "First off, I'll ask those of you who are armed to surrender your weapons at once. We'll start with you, lieutenant."

The police officer, embarrassed by the public recognition, took a pistol from an inner coat pocket and slid it across the floor to a place at Karl's feet.

"Thank you, sir," Karl said crisply. "Your turn, Domino."

The middle-aged gang leader feigned indignation, his eyes boring into his hireling as if to say, "No nonsense from you. Do your job the way I told you." But he at last produced his pistol and got rid of it in the same way as the police lieutenant.

"I'll appreciate the contributions of any other firearms or knives that any of you may be carrying," Karl went on jovially. "Believe me, my friends, it will be to your advantage to get rid of your weapons now. I'm inclined to become nasty—in fact, I develop a terrible itch in my trigger finger—when I discover that someone is still armed. So no funny business. I've got my eye on everyone in the room. One false move and I shoot the first person who doesn't do as I say."

The two card dealers relieved themselves of knives, and several of the other patrons got rid of pistols.

Karl circled the chamber slowly, relieving each

individual of cash. He refused to take any jewelry from either the ladies or the men, reasoning that he would need to call on an accomplice in order to rid himself of the gems. He well could be identified and brought to justice if he began to deal in stolen jewels.

Karl deliberately waited until he had robbed all of the other patrons before he approached Domino again. It had galled him to think that he had been asked to surrender the better part of his booty to the gang leader. His plan, however, would ensure that he was beholden to no one, and he was so confident of his luck and his ability that he had no fear of reprisals from any of Domino's men. Indeed, Kellerman even believed it was also possible that he might be able to take over many of the lucrative functions of the gang leader's organization.

For a few seconds his resolve faltered as Domino's steely eyes bored into him. But at last he said, "All right, it's your turn now."

The gang leader dug into his trousers pocket and dug out a thick roll of money. "Here," he said gruffly, dropping the money into Karl's hand.

As Karl stashed the money away in his own pocket, Domino began to search elsewhere. "I've got some more that I can give you," he said.

This was just the opportunity Karl needed. "I warned you what would happen if anybody tried to reach for a hidden gun," he said stridently, and was about to shoot when a woman standing nearby screamed. Karl was momentarily unnerved, but he still squeezed the trigger.

Domino staggered and crumpled to the floor, then lay still in a pool of blood.

His mission brilliantly accomplished, Karl lost no time in taking himself elsewhere. Flinging open the door, he raced down the steps two and three at a time, knocking the guard at the entrance to one side and tearing the bandanna from his face as he dashed out into the street. He ran to the curb, where several carriage drivers awaited possible fares. Leaping into the carriage at the head of the line, he promised the driver a double fee if the man would shake all pursuers.

They started at once for the center of town, and the driver was so adept that no one succeeded in following him. Karl kept his word and paid the man a double fare, then darted around the corner and caught another carriage for hire, which took him close to the waterfront. Discharging his second driver, he walked rapidly by a circuitous route to Dugald's Bar, where he unlocked the door and let himself in. He was much relieved when a quick glance in the cellar revealed that Wallace and the other victims were precisely where he had left them, still unconscious.

He had barely reemerged on the main floor when Robin Kayross arrived, accompanied by several of his loyal crew members, one of whom was driving a cart. The four unconscious men, Wallace Dugald among them, were taken from the cellar and piled into the cart, and an oilcloth cover was used to conceal them.

This was no time for conversation. Kayross handed

the former sergeant thirty-two hundred dollars in cash, then disappeared with his shanghaied cargo. Now at last Karl had the time to count his gains from the night's spoils. He was astonished to discover that his haul from the gaming establishment was far larger than he had anticipated: He had taken in thousands of dollars in return for one night's efforts. Now he could start living the life he craved, buying expensive clothes, eating only in the town's finest restaurants, and continuing to lead Millicent Randall on while making a play for both the luscious blonde and the expensive redhead who had interested him. By displaying courage and presence of mind, in one night he had assured his future.

Wallace Dugald's head ached, and he felt a tremendous thirst as he awakened. Little by little he became aware of his surroundings. He was lying on a filthy, foul-smelling mattress, and near the upper end was a container. The odor told him it was a chamber pot. The floor was made of metal and was filthy with a thick coating of coal dust. Nearby, something glowed inside an open door, and he finally realized it was a huge boiler of some kind. The heat was almost unbearable, and there was no daylight, no fresh air.

More to the point, he became conscious of his own predicament. A thick iron band encircled his right ankle, and he was chained to a stanchion from which he could move only a few feet in any direction.

As he watched, a small group of short, brown-skinned men appeared and began to shovel coal into the furnace. As the proprietor of a bar frequented by seamen, Wallace had become accustomed to judging men from all over the world, and he took it from their coloration and facial features that these men were Malays and Lascars.

The men—who were wearing loose-fitting, Western-style trousers but no shirts because of the heat—were not chained, and he called out to them eagerly, "You there! Where am I, and what's the meaning of these chains?"

There was no reply as the brown-skinned men went about their work.

Captain Robin Kayross approached, wearing the cap and jacket whose faded, tarnished gold braid symbolized his authority. In one hand he carried a short, ugly cat-o'-nine-tails. "You're awake, I see," he said.

"That I am," Wallace replied, "and I demand to know the meaning of this outrage. Why am I chained in this awful place?"

Kayross lashed out and struck him full across the face with the whip. "You'll address me as 'sir,' " he said, "and you'll speak to me respectfully because that's due my rank. Do I make myself clear?"

Wallace was infuriated, but the blood oozing from a cut the whip had inflicted on his upper lip served as a reminder that he had no choice. "Yes, sir," he said.

"That's more like it," Kayross said. "Just keep in mind that you'll be whipped into obedience any time you start acting up. You're lucky you weren't killed, you know. But you look smart enough to do what you're told to stay alive."

The man looked familiar, and all at once, Wallace placed him. He was a sea captain who had spent long hours in the Dugald Bar drinking and talking in low tones with Karl Kellerman. Suddenly he remembered that Karl had drugged him, and he put the whole picture together. Karl had rendered him helpless and then delivered him into the hands of this equally unscrupulous fellow.

"I intend taking no chances and being forced to shoot you because you were trying to escape. You're staying right where you are until we put out to sea, and if you behave yourself, your chains will then be removed, and you can move to the fo'c'sle with the rest of the crew. In the meantime, you'll keep the engine stoked like it is now; that way, we're ready to take off and put out to sea any time we want. You'll obey my officers, or you'll get the hide ripped off you. I find that when common sense fails, one language my indentured seamen always understand is the langugae of the whip." He swished the cat-o'-nine-tails back and forth. "Do what you're told when you're told to do it, and you'll be fed two meals a day," Kayross said. "I hope I make myself clear."

"Very clear, sir," Wallace replied, digging his fingernails into the palms of his hands. No one would ever know the great effort that his docility cost him.

Kayross grunted and then called out to the Lascars and Malays who were lurking in the shadows.

"Let the fate of this miserable one be a lesson to you," he said to them. "Do that which is expected of you, and you will be well treated. Disobey me and my officers, and you will be reduced to the level of this poor slave. For your own good, remember my words!" Not bothering to glance again in the direction of Wallace, he stamped off and left the furnace room.

For a long moment, no one stirred or spoke. Then one of the Malays obtained a cup of cool water from somewhere and handed it to Wallace. The gesture was so unexpected that Wallace's voice was husky as he thanked the man. Taking the cup, he drained it in order to relieve his burning thirst. Turning away, he picked up a shovel lying on the floor next to his dirty pallet, and thrusting it into the nearest pile of coal, he began to feed the furnace.

His mind racing as he thought about the dilemma in which he found himself, he worked until his torn shirt was wet with sweat and clung to his body. Rivulets of perspiration descended from his forehead and burned his eyes, but he merely blinked them away. He was lost in thought, and as he and the brown-skinned men kept the furnace burning up to the point that Captain Kayross had specified, he was seething with anger at his partner, who had no doubt sold him for a handsome sum. Now he faced a miserable existence as a common seaman, and unless he behaved in an exemplary manner, he would be severely punished.

Gazing into the fire with eyes that blazed like

the coal flames burning there, he spoke in a voice that throbbed with emotion. "If I could," he said aloud, "I'd break these chains and smash them over the head of my double-crossing partner. I've lost the gold that I accumulated through long hours of work, and with it, my half-interest in the saloon that was my whole life. I'm condemned to an existence that will be the death of me if I don't watch my step.

"But I intend to live! No matter what may happen, I'll stay alive and protect myself. Above all else on earth, I crave revenge against Karl Kellerman." Ordinarily shy and mild-mannered, he spoke now with a soul-shattering intensity that seemed to shake the metal floor of the furnace room.

"So help me God," he declared, "I will obtain vengeance against Karl Kellerman if it's the last thing on earth that I ever do!" He shook his fist in the light of the furnace, and his shadow leaped high against the bulkhead. "I'll do anything that's needed," he swore. "If I must, I'll even sell my soul to the devil, but I will obtain vengeance!"

The changes in Karl Kellerman were so pronounced that Millicent Randall was deeply concerned. He was no longer the devoted suitor, the loving companion with whom she had left St. Louis and, compromising her whole future, had accompanied to New Orleans. More often than not, he behaved like a total stranger. He had been transformed into a man who spent increasingly vast sums of money on a stunning wardrobe with which no other man in New

Orleans could compete. Instead of accompanying her
on her shopping expeditions and escorting her to
dinner and supper at the finer restaurants of the
town, he now left her to her own devices. He seemed
to think that as long as he provided her with money
for her shopping excursions and meals, nothing further was required of him.

On several occasions, her confusion and loneli-
ness had impelled her to accept dinner invitations
from Jean-Pierre, but she preferred to avoid the
young French heir. It was plain that Jean-Pierre was
infatuated with her, but she didn't feel free to accept
his attentions. True, Karl was indifferent to her, but
she still loved him and even still hoped that someday
they might marry. What was more, she was afraid
Karl would take it quite amiss if she were to spend
her time with another man, let alone one as handsome and gallant as Jean-Pierre.

Karl, however, felt no similar inhibitions, telling
Millicent daily that his work was responsible for his
absences. Several evenings each week his work kept
him busy all night, and he did not return to the hotel
suite until midmorning the following day. Then he
only appeared long enough to bathe and change his
clothes, have breakfast with Millicent, then leave
again. Meanwhile, he paid court to the lovely blonde
with whom he had become acquainted at the restaurant. When she resisted his advances, however, he
began to lay siege to the red-haired beauty he had
also seen, and here he was far more successful. Within
a short period of time, thanks to the many gifts that

he lavished upon her, he was engaged in a violent affair with her.

Millicent had no way of knowing where he went or who accompanied him, but she began to grow suspicious. On several occasions she thought she smelled perfume on the clothes he left for the laundress.

This particular morning began like so many others that had preceded it. After having eaten breakfast in the dining room of the Louisiana House, Millicent and Karl returned to their suite, where he meticulously adjusted his expensive new cravat in the mirror and took a flower from a fresh bunch in a vase to put in his lapel buttonhole.

"You'll have to keep yourself occupied today," he said. "I'm afraid I'm going to be tied up at work."

Something within Millicent rebelled, but she made no reply.

He reached into a pocket and peeled off a one-hundred-dollar bill from a wad of notes. "This is in case you find something that strikes your fancy while you're shopping. I suggest you eat your noon dinner here and charge the meal to the suite."

"What will you be doing?" she demanded, unable to control her fury. "Eating dinner in a private room somewhere with your romance of the moment?"

Karl retreated at once into a hard shell. "I beg your pardon," he said distinctly. "I prefer to ignore that comment, and I would rather pretend that you never said it."

She had gone too far to stop now; her suspicions

were getting the better of her. "You aren't nearly as clever as you like to believe," she said hotly. "You've succeeded in convincing yourself that you've had me badly fooled, but you haven't. I think I could name the exact date that you started cheating on me."

Karl feigned great indignation. "I've told you many times that I have business to conduct," he shouted angrily. "If you don't want to believe me, that's your prerogative, and you're free to walk out on me whenever you wish. But what will you do then? You'll have no money and nowhere to go. That means you'll wind up in the only place that's open to you—one of the many brothels for which New Orleans is noted."

Millicent, suddenly frightened at the picture he painted, began to weep.

Karl reached out and slapped her hard across the face. "Your tears won't win you any sympathy from me," he said harshly. "Stop that crying!"

Not knowing that the sight of feminine tears drove him into a frenzy, she wept still harder. Suddenly he reached out, caught hold of one of her wrists, and twisted her arm behind her back. "Damn you!" he shouted. "I told you to stop crying!"

She thought he intended to wrench her arm from its socket. The pain was excruciating, but she managed, somehow, to stem the flow of tears.

Having resorted to physical abuse, Karl was incapable of stopping. He twisted her arm still harder, and moaning because of the intense pain, she collapsed onto the bed.

"I go when and where I please," he told her roughly. "Hereafter, you'll keep your thoughts on the subject to yourself, and if you don't like what I'm doing, you'll still smile and keep up a front as though you're enjoying life with me. I have no intention of supporting you if you're going to complain all the time, make life miserable for me, and get yourself all red-eyed in the process."

Grinding her teeth together until her jaw ached, Millicent continued to stifle her sobs.

"Be glad I don't throw you out into the street," he said. "From now on, be grateful for any attention that I may pay you, and act accordingly. I expect you to be ingenious in the ways that you display your gratitude to me." He gave her arm a final, excruciating wrench. Then, after examining himself in the mirror, he left the suite, slamming the door behind him.

Burying her face in her pillow, Millicent gave in to her feelings and wept at length, sobbing hard. Ultimately, she cried herself out, then, rising dully, went to her dressing table, where she removed all her cosmetics. In her misery, she had forgotten all about Jean-Pierre's offers of kindness, and she believed she had no one to advise her, nowhere to go for help. She felt totally trapped. She would be forced to do as Karl had demanded and go along with whatever he did, pretending that she liked it. Never had her future seemed so bleak.

*   *   *

The house was located in an old, middle-class, Creole section of New Orleans and had a wrought-iron balcony on the second floor overlooking a small, informal garden. The balcony opened onto a large, simply furnished chamber, and into it, carrying a tray of food, came a hard-faced young man who was unaccustomed to the role of nurse that he was being obliged to play.

"Here's your noon dinner, Domino," he said. "It ain't much with all that mush in it, but we're fixing exactly what the doctor said you could have."

Domino, his face pale, his head swathed in bandages, struggled to a sitting position in the four-poster bed. "I'm grateful for every bite of food the doctors allow me to eat," he said. "I'm gathering strength day by day, and that's all that matters."

"I'm sure you're right, boss," the young man replied, placing the tray in his superior's lap.

"I get chills," Domino said as he began to eat, "every time I think of that woman's scream deflecting Kellerman's aim. Another quarter of an inch and the bullet would have gone into my brain and finished me. That was as close a call as I'll ever have." He shuddered and ate more rapidly.

The younger man shifted his weight uncomfortably from foot to foot. He was under instructions to discuss whatever Domino wished to talk about, with one exception. Under no circumstances was he to refer to the incident in which the gang leader had almost lost his life. He had no idea what he was to do when Domino insisted on raising the subject himself.

The older man grimaced as he downed a glass of fruit juice. "I wonder how soon the doctors will let me have some whiskey to drink again," he said, and his sigh hung in the air.

His young associate knew the question required no answer and was relieved.

The gang leader quickly finished his meal, devouring every bite of the food. He was behaving like a model patient because he knew that the more closely he followed the orders of his physician, the sooner he would enjoy a complete recovery.

As the young man took the lunch tray and left the room, Domino sat back and reflected how he would repay Karl Kellerman for his treachery. The gang leader had begun by instructing his associates to keep completely mum in regard to the state of their employer's health following the shocking incident in the gambling hall; that way no one would know if Domino was alive or dead. He wanted Karl Kellerman to spend his days in a fool's paradise, thinking he had disposed of the crime leader, when in the meantime Domino would be planning ways to dispose of Kellerman that would cause him the most prolonged agony possible. Domino didn't yet know exactly what he would do to the man, but when the time was right, Karl Kellerman would suffer the tortures of the damned.

IV

Edward Blackstone had booked passage for his party on board the *Mississippi Lady*, an elegant paddle-wheeler that was a combined passenger and cargo ship. Ordinarily the voyage from Memphis to New Orleans on such a vessel would have been a delight from beginning to end, but Edward was too preoccupied and too anxious to find Karl Kellerman. Consequently, he was in no mood to enjoy the serene beauty of the journey down the Mississippi, nor could he appreciate the delights of such river towns as Natchez and Baton Rouge.

Tommie made no attempts to persuade Edward to relax. She was aware of his single-minded devotion to duty, and she recognized his need to find Millicent and to persuade her to give up the abandoned life that she was leading. Until he achieved that goal, everything else was secondary to him.

Even Edward's constant companion, Robin Hood, the little monkey dressed to resemble the hero of the

British legend of the Middle Ages, failed to amuse
Edward these days. So Tommie paid more attention
to the animal than she usually did, took care of his
feeding, and kept him with her for long periods.

At last, the party arrived in New Orleans and
went straight to their hotel. While they were settling
into their rooms, Edward went down to the lobby
and consulted with a hotel employee as to the whereabouts of Dugald's Bar, which he proposed to visit
that same night. He got directions on how to get to
the place, and then he returned to the suite that he
and his companions occupied. Jim and Randy awaited
him in the parlor.

"I think," Edward said to them, "that we should
eat an early supper tonight."

"Good," Jim replied.

"Then we can set out immediately for the saloon
that Karl Kellerman owns," Randy proposed.

Edward shook his head. "I'm sorry to disappoint
you, gentlemen, especially after you've traveled such
a great distance in order to help recover Millicent,
but as I mentioned, I believe I should face Kellerman
alone at this first meeting. Since I've met him
previously, I think I know a little something about
him. I don't want this initial meeting to get his back
up. I'm sure I'll accomplish a great deal more if I go
to him calmly, and quietly inquire about Millicent's
whereabouts. If it should prove necessary, then you
shall certainly come with me to a second meeting,
but I hope that it won't be necessary."

Jim Randall smiled ruefully and fingered the

butt of the Colt repeating pistol that he carried in a holster on his belt. "I've got to admit that I'm disappointed, Edward, and that I've been spoiling for a fight with the no-good rotter who ran off with Millicent without marrying her. But I agree that it's better if he cooperates with us voluntarily rather than by our using fists and firearms, so I suppose that means that I've got to back off and give you the benefit of a first meeting with the devil alone."

"I'll be on my guard, never fear," Edward told them, "and thank you for your confidence, gentlemen. I can assure you that I won't let you down."

The door that led to Tommie Harding's bedchamber opened, and the young woman, who had already changed into a simple but attractive black dress for supper, came into the parlor. Jim and Randy, reasoning that she and Edward might want to spend some time alone, discreetly retired to the room that they shared.

"You look lovely this evening," Edward told her when they were by themselves.

She inclined her head demurely. "Thank you, sir." Then she hastened to add, "I think this dress will be quite appropriate for our meeting tonight with Kellerman."

"Whether or not the dress is appropriate is a moot point," he said. "As I mentioned earlier, I don't want anyone coming with me."

Tommie looked as though he had slapped her across the face. "I don't understand," she said. "I know Kellerman every bit as well as you do. After the death of de Cordova, when he was still a police officer, Kellerman spent a long time interrogating me on my father's boat. I also spoke to him at length at supper that same night."

"I can't deny anything you've said," Edward told her, "but all the same, this isn't a social occasion. I'm calling on Kellerman to settle a serious matter, and he's got to be made to recognize the validity of my demand. If you come with me, the whole tenor of the meeting will be different. I want you to stay right here in the hotel and not budge from this suite until I get back. From all I've heard, New Orleans can be a very tough town for a woman alone, and if I'm forced to leave your side tonight for any reason, you'd be totally unprotected."

"You sound," she said indignantly, "as though I've spent my whole life in cotton batting. I'll have you know that I've traveled up and down the Missouri River with my father, visiting every town on the water, and by that I mean every rough frontier community. I can assure you they're all a darn sight tougher and nastier than New Orleans. Relatively speaking, this is a community for ladies and gentlemen, and I can promise you, I get along here just fine!"

Edward had enough problems on his mind without being forced to worry about Tommie's welfare, too. "You may be perfectly right," he said. "The streets of New Orleans may be as safe as those in London, but all the same, I want you to stay indoors tonight and not to leave the hotel, and I expect you to abide by my word."

Tommie became infuriated. "What gives you the right to give me orders?" she demanded.

Edward controlled his own temper with a great effort. "My concern for your safety and well-being gives me every right to look after you," he said, "and to ask you in the name of common sense to behave yourself. It was only with the gravest reservations that I allowed you to accompany me even this far in the first place." His tone softened, and he took her hands in his. "I'm not regretting for a moment that you're here; I love you, and I want you with me all the time. If I thought it was to our advantage to take you with me, I'd certainly take you with me tonight. Under the circumstances, however, I find nothing to be gained. Be good enough to reconcile yourself to the need to stay here in the hotel, safe and sound, and to keep Robin Hood company during the few hours that I'll be gone!"

Tommie said nothing, but inside she was still seething about Edward's command to remain in the hotel suite all evening. Having acted as chief of her father's crew on countless Missouri River voyages, she had enjoyed a measure of independence rare to most women in the age in which she lived. She had learned to take care of herself when danger threatened, and consequently, she vowed that nothing would stop her from following Edward when he went out to see Karl Kellerman.

They ate their dinner in the hotel dining room, and as soon as Edward left them—with Jim and Randy heading for the card room to enjoy a game of

poker while they waited for Edward's return—Tommie
went up to their suite and quickly threw a long, dark
gray cape over her shoulders. Before she could get
out the door, however, Robin Hood leaped onto one
shoulder and clung to her. It was impossible for her
to disengage the animal quickly, so she had to make
the best of things by allowing the monkey to accompany her. If she took time to pry him loose and leave
him in the suite, Edward would be out of sight by
the time she reached the street.

So with the little monkey—clad in a green dou-
blet and a matching hat with a jaunty feather in
it—clinging to her shoulder, Tommie followed Edward and, staying in the shadows, made her way
behind him toward the waterfront district. Neither
Tommie nor Edward knew it, of course, but Millicent Randall had every intention of following Karl
Kellerman that same night and determining to her
own satisfaction whether he was being unfaithful to
her or whether he was really engaging in business.
After his abusive treatment of her that morning, she
had spent a long, introspective day and had ultimately concluded that she needed specific information if she was to take action of any kind. She had to
admit that most of the evidence she had accumulated
to prove Karl's infidelity was circumstantial. She
merely assumed—but did not know for certain—that
he was seeing another woman.

In the back of Millicent's mind, a loose plan was
taking shape. If Karl indeed proved unfaithful to her,
she would slip away and would join Jean-Pierre

Gautier, who, she now saw clearly, would be delighted to help her in every possible way. Jean-Pierre had indicated that he believed Karl was unworthy of her, although he had never said anything specific against him, but his own interest in her was sufficiently great that she knew he would take her in, give her shelter, and provide her with whatever funds she needed. At the very least, she reflected, she had an alternative and was not reduced to sitting in her bedchamber at the Louisiana House wringing her hands helplessly while Karl cavorted with some other woman.

Early that evening, Karl had returned briefly to their hotel suite to wash up and put on some expensive cologne. Millicent was not surprised when he said he was required to go elsewhere on business and that she was to eat supper alone in the hotel dining room. She agreed so quickly and meekly that he was convinced he had taught her a lesson that morning when he had abused her.

Instead of doing as he had bidden, however, she gave him a head start of only a few seconds and then silently followed him into the corridor and down the stairs. She had dressed with special care in a dark, unadorned dress, which she wore with black shoes and stockings. Over her gown she threw a short, dark cloak.

Fortunately Karl was in no hurry and took his time as he sauntered down the street and headed toward the wharves. Millicent followed him at a safe distance and had no difficulty in keeping pace with him. She raised an eyebrow when she saw the neighborhood becoming shabbier, for she had assumed that he was so fastidious that any woman with whom he chose to associate would have a background of wealth, breeding, and culture.

Various male passersby who saw Millicent heading down the street immediately assumed that she was a prostitute and made verbal advances to her. Terrified, she ignored them.

At last Karl came to Dugald's Bar, which he had been keeping closed during the day, ever since Wallace had been shanghaied. He unlocked the door, entered, and lighted the gas lamps. Taking off his expensive suit jacket and rolling up his sleeves, he went behind the bar and began wiping down the counter with a rag.

Two men now entered the bar and greeted Karl boisterously. Millicent, surreptitiously watching the exchange through the window, had no way of knowing that the pair were Karl's henchmen, both of whom were addicted to opium and depended on him for the money to buy the drug. As a result, they did whatever he wished.

Millicent caught her breath as two other patrons who had been awaiting the opening of the establishment for the night made their appearance and Karl served them. Watching him as he prepared their drinks, the woman felt faint. Karl's regular, frequent absences from her company were not caused by his attentions to another woman. They were due exclusively to the fact that he was working in a saloon called Dugald's Bar.

Now Millicent was convinced she knew why he had become so angry when she had accused him of being unfaithful to her. He had been badly hurt, and she could not blame him for feeling as he had. She felt certain she had accused him falsely.

Karl had concealed his vocation from her because he had not wanted her to know that he was earning a living doing menial work. Obviously he wanted her to believe that he was plentifully supplied with funds through his various business connections and had no need to do a common laborer's work in order to support them in style. Her heart overflowed with gratitude to him, and at that moment, she loved him more than ever before. Closing her eyes and leaning against the building for support, Millicent was almost overcome by feelings of tenderness for Karl. Not only had she misjudged him, she thought, but he had been motivated in all he had done only by his love for her.

The two patrons who had entered earlier left the premises, and a husky, young cargo handler came in, sat down at the bar, and ordered himself an ale. As Karl turned away to fill his glass, he exchanged swift glances with his two henchmen, who were seated nearby. The newcomer was a splendid specimen and would be a perfect recruit for Robin Kayross, who would be paying Dugald's Bar another visit that same evening.

Karl promptly slipped some knockout drops into

the new arrival's mug and then pushed it across the bar to him. The young man took a few swallows and soon became woozy. Immediately thereafter, he lost consciousness.

As he slumped forward on his stool, sprawling across the bar, Karl signaled to his two confederates. Knowing what was to be done, they were on their feet instantly. They opened the trapdoor to the cellar, carried the unconcious cargo handler down the rickety staircase, then bound him securely hand and foot.

At that moment Millicent entered Dugald's Bar, unaware of what had just taken place, thinking only how wonderful Karl was.

Karl caught his breath and gaped at her. Talking rapidly, she apologized to him profusely for her suspicions, which she admitted were groundless, and she thanked him at length for working to support her while concealing his vocation from her. Relieved by her ignorance, Karl eagerly accepted her interpretation of events and played his part to the hilt. "I'm glad you understand at last," he said. "I'm sorry that I had to get rough with you this morning—"

"Oh, I understand!" Millicent cried, "and I don't blame you in the least."

Karl allowed her to hug him briefly before he led her to a table situated in a far corner at the rear of the room. "I'll get you a cup of coffee. Just be sure you stay out of the way while you're drinking it. I don't want any customers who come in here to think that you're available to them for purposes of their own, so pay no attention to anyone and mind your own business."

"Oh, I will," she said.

"It well may be several hours before I'll have the opportunity to escort you back to the hotel," he said. "As you can imagine, I'm more or less stuck here. Until then, I want you well out of the way."

"Don't worry about me," Millicent told him. "I've already caused you enough troubles, and I'll be very good until you're ready to leave."

He seated her at the corner table, half facing the wall, where she would be unaware if any other customers encountered the same fate as the cargo handler. The thought occurred to Karl that if the need arose, Millicent, in her innocence, could provide him with the perfect alibi for his own evening's activities; he could turn her unexpected appearance to his own advantage.

Millicent sat meekly at the rear corner table, quietly accepting the cup of coffee that Karl brought her and, her eyes downcast, paid no attention to his two henchmen when they returned from the cellar where they had deposited the cargo handler.

Watching Millicent as she sipped her coffee, Karl reflected that his luck was good. He was leading a charmed life; it appeared that he could do no wrong.

Edward Blackstone had no idea that he was being followed, so it didn't occur to him to turn and look back. He was not in a hurry, and as he went out into the busy streets of New Orleans, Tommie had no difficulty in following a short distance behind.

As the neighborhood changed block by block, she became uneasy and was annoyed with herself because she had failed to take any weapons. She discovered that she was strangely comforted by the presence on her shoulder of Robin Hood. The little monkey could offer her scant protection if some stranger assaulted her, but at least the animal was company of some kind.

Eventually Edward reached his destination. Pausing to peer in through the window, he saw Karl Kellerman very much alive and in command of himself and his surroundings, standing behind the bar. Millicent was nowhere in view because the table at which she sat was just out of sight from the window.

Edward now went into the saloon. Tommie immediately moved forward and replaced him at the window.

When he saw Edward, Kellerman instantly realized that the Englishman was searching for his cousin, and that once he found her, he would try to learn about Kellerman's affairs. His mind racing, Kellerman knew he could not tolerate an investigation, which might unmask him and send him to prison.

Instantly alert, Kellerman called out softly to his two henchmen, who were sitting at the far end of the bar. "See that tall, fancy dude standing in the entrance?" he demanded. "He's dangerous! Knock him out and dispose of him, but be careful. He's likely to do you some real damage if he suspects you're after him."

Millicent turned and was electrified when she saw Edward standing in the doorway. She heard the instructions that Karl gave the pair at the bar, and though she had no idea what Karl was up to, she now realized that her original instinct had been right: Whatever it was, Karl was up to no good. Clearly Edward had made this surprise appearance at Dugald's Bar in order to find her, and Karl was determined to prevent him from achieving his goal.

Jumping to her feet and moving forward, Millicent began to signal frantically to Edward, warning him to beware of the two men at the bar. Her gestures were plain to Tommie, who was watching the developing scene outside the window. Edward, however, misinterpreted her signals. He was not suffering from any lack of alertness, but he was so delighted to see Millicent that he thought she actually appeared to be welcoming him, and he started to go toward her.

Tommie wanted to cry out as the pair at the bar separated and began to rush Edward from behind.

Millicent's signals became frantic, and she called out, "Edward! Edward, look . . ." Ignoring Kellerman at the bar, Edward continued heading toward her.

Tommie was paralyzed by fright, her heart rising to her mouth as she watched one of the pair, armed with a length of leather-covered lead pipe, strike Edward sharply across the back of the head. He became unconscious and sagged to the floor.

The pair caught hold of him, and producing lengths of rope, they expertly began to bind his ankles and wrists. They relieved him of his pistol and found under his coat jacket the little derringer he kept concealed there. As a final touch, they tied a gag around his mouth. Then, still moving swiftly, one of them opened the trapdoor to the cellar. Then rejoining his companion, he and the other man picked up Edward, carried his unconscious body down to the foot of the rickety staircase, then came up again and carefully closed the trapdoor behind them.

Millicent was so stunned that she was incapable of moving. When she looked at Karl, she saw an unfathomable expression in his eyes, and something in his smile made her blood run cold.

"If you'd stayed at the Louisiana Hotel, as I told you to do," he said, "you wouldn't be in any trouble right now. But you were curious, and now you've found out far more than is good for you. You may find it hard to believe this, but I have nothing personal against you. Unfortunately for you, however, you know enough to create one hell of a lot of trouble for me in the wrong places, so I've got to protect myself. I hope you'll understand." He turned to his two henchmen. "Tie her up, gag her, and put her downstairs, boys," he said. "But there's no need for any rough games with her. She won't put up any fight. Treat her gently while I figure out what's to be done with her."

The men turned to her immediately, and she offered them no resistance as they tied her hands and feet and tied a gag around her mouth. Then they opened the trapdoor again and, between them, carried her down the precariously wobbly staircase to the cellar below. There the horrified Millicent saw Edward and a stranger trussed and gagged, both of them lying unconscious on the floor. The henchmen exchanged a look, and instead of stretching her out on the cement floor beside their other victims, they propped her against the nearest wall and left her in a standing position.

Then the trapdoor above closed again, and Millicent was plunged into darkness.

Tommie Harding, still peering in surreptitiously through the window, faced a terrible dilemma. Seeing Kellerman's hirelings return to the main floor of the bar after depositing Millicent below, she realized that the same fate quite possibly awaited her if she revealed her presence. What could a lone, unarmed woman and a small monkey possibly do against two armed thugs and Kellerman?

Equally to the point, she was in a part of New Orleans that was totally alien to her, and she could wander aimlessly for a long time before she stumbled onto the nearest police headquarters. Common sense told her that neither Edward nor Millicent would be held indefinitely in the cellar of Dugald's Bar; eventually they would be moved elsewhere. Therefore, if she left now and sought help from the police, there well might be no sign of either her fiancé or his cousin in the bar by the time she returned. Knowing Kellerman, she realized that he could swear to the authorities that he had seen neither Edward nor Millicent, and there would be no way on earth that she could prove she was telling the truth.

Consequently, she had to stay and keep watch, no matter what happened. It was the only way that she could try to protect Edward and his cousin. Wherever they were taken, she would follow them there, and perhaps then she would have a better chance to summon the help of the police.

Tommie suddenly realized that a passerby had halted, and she tried to shrink against the wall adjacent to the saloon's window. However, the man sauntered closer, studying her carefully. She didn't want to look directly at him but was able to make out that he was wearing seamen's garb.

"How are you tonight?" he asked, his English slightly accented.

Tommie made no reply.

"You look very lonely," he said, coming still closer.

"You've made a mistake, sir," Tommie said, addressing a point in space above and behind him. "I'm not the type of woman you appear to think me."

The sailor laughed easily. "All I'm thinking," he replied, "is that you're very pretty and very lonely." He reached out tentatively for her.

Conquering the feeling of panic that welled up within her, Tommie drew back. "I must beg you to be careful," she said desperately. "My monkey has been trained, and he will scratch your eyes out."

The sailor laughed derisively. Robin Hood heard

the man's derogatory tone, felt the tension in the air, and began to grimace and chatter angrily.

"There, you see?" Tommie demanded. "There's nothing I can do to stop him." The monkey continued to chatter even more rapidly.

The sailor looked dubious. He had no desire to test the animal, however, and so he reluctantly drew back, stared at Tommie for another instant or two, then turned on his heel and made his way down the street. Tommie stroked the animal's head softly. "That was wonderful, Robin," she whispered, "just wonderful."

Pressing close to the outside wall of the saloon, Tommie peered through a corner of the dusty window and saw Kellerman and his henchmen laughing boisterously. She found herself praying that they would move Edward and Millicent soon. Since she alone knew of their plight, she alone was in a position to save them. No matter how dangerous, she had to stick out her mission to the finish.

Toby Holt planned to pay a visit to San Francisco in order to confer with Chet Harris and Wong Ke, the enormously successful businessmen who controlled so many enterprises on the Pacific coast. They knew more about the existence and activities of the tongs than did anyone else, and he wanted to learn whatever he could from them.

On the eve of his departure from the Portland area, his wife Clarissa gave a small dinner party. The guests included his sister Cindy and his closest friend and business associate, Rob Martin. With Rob came his second wife, Kale, a reformed courtesan who was a stunning beauty, with violet eyes and long blue-black hair gathered in a bun at the nape of her neck.

They drank glasses of sherry before supper, and Kale dominated the conversation. "You don't know," she said, "how fortunate we are to be living in the American West, where people are taking advantage of the trend toward women's suffrage."

"You're right, Kale. State universities are opening their doors to women now," Cindy said. "Eventually the movement may spread all over the country."

"The success of women's suffrage is so great it can't be reversed," Kale said. "People like Susan B. Anthony, Elizabeth Cady Stanton, and Lucy Stone—who has flatly refused to take her husband's name of Blackwell—are leading what has become a positive crusade."

"How far do you expect women to carry their crusade?" Toby asked.

"The frontiers are unlimited," Kale replied. "Once women start being educated on an equal basis with men, they'll enter the professions. There'll be lady doctors and lady lawyers, as well as teachers. In various states here in the West, women can already vote on such matters as local bond issues and local taxation. Laugh if you want to, but I predict that the day isn't that far distant when we'll have universal female suffrage."

"I'm in favor of it," Toby said. "The way I see this thing is that any woman who wants to can learn as much about national and international issues as any man."

"Hear, hear!" his wife said.

"You're being awfully quiet, Rob," Kale said. "Do you disagree with us?"

Tall, red-haired Rob Martin swirled his glass of sherry, seemingly lost in thought. At last he replied, "It's not that I disagree with what you're all saying. It's just that you, Kale, have come a long way. You have traveled a hard road in order to win acceptance from the people of Portland, and I hate to see you setting yourself back. Some men have no use for women's suffrage, and I hate to see them taking out their anger on you."

"If they do," Kale said with spirit, "it's because they're shortsighted and ignorant of what's at stake. It isn't accidental, you know, that I've become a champion of women's suffrage. When I was a girl I was terribly ambitious, and my family had nothing—no money and no influence. I knew of only one path I could follow to become relatively well off financially and attain a measure of power, if not prestige. I became a prostitute. Oh, I hated myself whenever I stopped to think about it, but my goal remained steady and unvarying. Obviously, I didn't obtain real peace of mind until I left my profession and married, but I'm damned if I want my stepdaughter—or any-one else's daughter—to suffer because she's a female. If we're really living in the land of the free—and I believe we are—let's prove it by giving our daugh-ters every opportunity that we offer to our sons!"

"You put it so well, Kale," Cindy said in admiration, "that you leave nothing for Clarissa or me to add. I'm glad I'm a woman, and I'm glad I am living in a time when we'll see the results of our fight for suffrage bear fruit."

"All I ask," Rob told her, "is that you do nothing to jeopardize the acceptance that you've struggled so hard to win."

"I agree to that," Kale said, "provided I do nothing to injure my self-respect. That comes first."

Her husband agreed, and everyone present thought the issue was resolved. No one had any idea of the problems that would face Kale in the months that stretched out ahead.

The following day, Toby left for San Francisco. The stagecoach ride from Portland was long and tiresome. Finally arriving he checked into his hotel and for once got a night's sleep after days on the road. Early the following day, he sat in the wood-paneled, richly furnished office of the millionaire Chet Harris, explaining all about the documents that incriminated Kung Lee's tong and that had been sent on to General Blake. Also present at the meeting was Chet's partner, Wong Ke. The big, somewhat over-weight Chet and the slight, ascetic-looking, elderly Chinese man made a strange pair. They had met years earlier during the California gold rush, had made a fortune together, and had become close friends as well as business partners.

Their offices were located on the heights overlooking San Francisco Bay, and as Toby listened to Ke, he looked at the magnificent panorama spread out below him.

"American society," Ke was saying, "is becoming increasingly industrialized and therefore more complex, so it stands to reason that as immigrants from other lands come here, they cling to old ways, many of them bad, as forms of self-protection. This is certainly true of the Chinese, who have transferred their powerful tongs, or secret protective societies, from Canton and Shanghai to the shores of North America."

"Have they always been as vicious as they are here?" Toby asked.

Wong Ke shook his head. "No," he said. "They began as secret patriotic societies during the Opium Wars with European powers. As our Chinese cities were occupied, the patriots went underground and opposed the rule of the foreign devils in private. Unfortunately, by the time the tongs spread across the Pacific, they were already involved in illegal activities and were using terrorist tactics to control people. The vicious beating they recently administered to me in Portland is typical of their methods. They have no place in America and serve no useful function in American society. I'm opposed to them and to their methods."

"Do they specialize in any types of illegal activity?" Toby asked.

The elderly Chinese man shook his head. "The

modern tong reaches out its tentacles into every phase of Chinese society in the United States. Nothing is immune to them, nothing escapes their interest. They earn large sums of money from the importation of opium and from illegal immigration. They collect extortion money from local merchants, and they have a stranglehold on prostitution and gambling in every Chinatown in America. They hound restaurant owners, and they try to intimidate businessmen like me. Unfortunately for them, I have a tough old hide, and I don't scare easily."

"What can you tell me," Toby asked, "about individual tongs?"

"There are several with headquarters in Canton and branches in such cities as Shanghai and Hong Kong, the British colony. Several have successfully managed the leap across the Pacific Ocean so far, but there is one that has most of the power, wealth, and influence in the United States. Its name is a closely guarded secret, and I don't think that the name matters much to outsiders. However, what matters is that the authorities now have in their possession the documents that were being delivered to General Blake, documents that could help implicate the tong in illegal activities. As you've learned, the head of the organization is a man named Kung Lee. We can tell you where to locate him—we have our own sources of information—but let me say that if and when you meet him for the first time, you'll be impressed by him as a cultured, witty, and sophisticated gentleman. But don't let his surface manner fool you. He has his delicate fingers in crimes of every sort, from illegal immigration to gambling and prostitution. He rules his empire with an iron hand. It's said that he's as powerful in his way as the dowager empress is in China, and to call the organization that he rules an empire is no exaggeration."

"He must indeed control a great fortune," Toby said.

Wong Ke nodded emphatically as he pressed his fingertips together. "That which Kung Lee rules," he said, "is truly an empire and worth many millions of dollars. No one knows exactly what its real worth is, just as no one really knows how extensive its roots extend beneath the surface of American society. All I know for certain is that Kung Lee's tong cannot be eradicated overnight. That's an impossible achievement."

Chet entered the conversation for the first time. "In order to better understand the makeup of the tong hierarchy," he said, "you've got to know that Kung Lee, like any absolute ruler, is surrounded by advisers, aides, bodyguards, and hatchet men. His person is regarded as almost sacred, and he has layers of helpers who shield him not only from the general public but from his enemies."

"Let me tell you, Toby, about Ho Tai, who is just one of Kung Lee's bodyguards," Ke said. "He's a burly, short, squat man, hideously ugly, and is the most dangerous of foes. I happen to know that he underwent long training as an assassin in Canton and in Hong Kong. He is responsible to no one but Kung Lee, and his one aim in life is do the bidding of his employer."

"I don't know whether Ho Tai has earned his notorious reputation," Chet interjected, "but he is said to be the most dangerous of hatchet men and the deadliest of knife throwers. He's allegedly killed many opponents. No one knows the exact number, and the stories are undoubtedly exaggerated. Nevertheless, he's a killer with a long list of victims."

"If his misdeeds are so well known," Toby said, "I'm surprised the authorities don't have him picked up and sent to prison."

"It has been impossible," Wong Ke said, "to gather any substantial evidence against the man. Witnesses are afraid to testify, and no one will speak up against him. He is known to enjoy the complete confidence and protection of Kung Lee, and that is all that he needs in order to do as he pleases."

"I can see where Mr. Kung Lee and I are headed on a collision course," Toby said, smiling grimly. "First, you were attacked, then my sister was attacked, and so was I. I think the time has come for me to meet Mr. Kung Lee face to face and exchange a few words with him."

Chet sighed. "I could close my eyes," he said, "and swear that I hear Whip Holt speaking. I thought he was the only man on earth who didn't know the meaning of fear and was prepared to step into a lion's den at a moment's notice, but he *wasn't* the only one. He has a son who is exactly like him, who also doesn't know the meaning of fear. I hate violence, and I shudder to think of what may happen when you and Kung Lee come face to face."

"I don't know if anyone has ever had the courage to tell him what people think of him," Toby said, "but we'll find out soon enough what happens when he's forced to listen to the truth!"

It was a typical morning in the Chinatown curio shop. Earlier, several tourists from the East Coast had visited the establishment and made predictable purchases of carved chopsticks and of pseudo–temple bells.

Quiet had reigned for an hour or two, and now a lone visitor wandered into the shop. Certainly he did not look like a tourist. In his late twenties and heavily bronzed as a result of spending the better part of his life outdoors, he was tall and sinewy. His broad-brimmed western hat rode on the back of his head, and his attire, from open-throated shirt to trousers stuffed into leather boots, indicated that he was a working westerner who probably lived on a ranch.

The handles of two knives protruded from his belt, which was filled with bullets. Two Colt .44 repeating pistols were hanging in their holsters. The weapons were not new, and it was apparent from a glance at the handles that they had seen much use.

Instead of examining the many objects for sale

piled up on the shelves in the shop, the stranger glanced around the place and then approached the old man who was ostensibly the proprietor. The Chinese man found himself looking into the palest blue eyes he had ever seen. They had a mesmeric quality and seemed to bore into him.

"I am here," Toby Holt announced, "to see Kung Lee."

The old man was stunned, and while he gestured feebly, his young companion raced out and hurried off up the stairs.

Toby, guessing the young man's destination, appeared in no hurry. He strolled around the shop, seeming completely at ease.

After a few minutes' wait, a short, squat Chinese man, his ugly face covered with scars, appeared in the door. "What you want?" he demanded.

Toby's expression did not change. "You must be Ho Tai," he said mildly.

The Chinese bodyguard's eyes gleamed malevolently, but he made no reply.

"I didn't come here to see you," Toby said, his tone still civil. "I made it very clear that the purpose of my visit is to see Kung Lee. Will you be good enough to tell him I'm here, please?"

Still saying nothing, Ho Tai flexed his fingers.

Toby remained pleasant, but a firm note crept into his voice. "I know that Kung Lee makes his headquarters in this building," he said. "I've also gone to the trouble of finding out that he's in town, so the chances are good that he's under this roof at this moment. I have no quarrel with you, nor with anyone, but I intend to see him. Be good enough to tell him that Toby Holt is here." His hands dropped to the butts of his pistols. "Tell him now," he suggested, a hint of urgency in his voice.

The old man backed away nervously and put a table laden with curios between himself and the other two men. He was ready to duck down to the floor in the event that a shooting match developed.

Ho Tai was in no way intimidated by Toby, but he was under standing instructions to preserve the facade of peace, if not peace itself. "I find out if Kung Lee see you," he announced, his tone surly, and without further ado he whirled and made his way up the stairs.

Watching him, Toby noted that the bodyguard was exceptionally light on his feet.

After a very brief wait, Ho Tai reappeared at the landing on the second floor. "You come now," he said.

Toby mounted the stairs under the bodyguard's watchful, alert gaze.

"You give me guns and knife," Ho Tai commanded, extending a hand.

Toby looked at him and laughed. "There is no way that I'll surrender my weapons," he said. "Wherever I go, they go."

Ho Tai backed down and continued to practice peace. Shrugging, he led the way down a narrow corridor on creaking floorboards and then stood aside when they came to a closed door at the end of the hallway. He knocked and, opening the door, rested one hand on the hilt of a light but deadly throwing knife that he carried in his belt.

Toby knew the bodyguard was ready to intervene instantly if it should prove necessary, but he paid no further attention to the man. Instead he concentrated on the Chinese man, apparently about sixty years of age, who sat behind a large desk. Attired in black mandarin robes, Kung Lee was smiling, his expression revealing none of his hatred for this unwanted visitor. He waved Toby to a chair opposite where he himself sat.

Keeping one hand on the hilt of his knife, Ho Tai moved to a convenient corner and stood within full view of the visitor's chair.

"Thank you for receiving me on such short notice, Mr. Kung," Toby said politely.

"Not at all," the tong leader said, maintaining an air of great civility. "I am honored that a man of your reputation should visit my humble office."

Toby discounted the compliment but nevertheless was gratified that Kung Lee had heard of him. Perhaps his reputation would make his present task somewhat easier.

"I've been looking forward to this meeting with you, Mr. Kung," he said. "I believe that a meeting of the minds will solve a number of potential problems."

"I am aware of no problems, Mr. Holt," Kung replied, and folded his hands.

"I try to take the long view," Toby said blandly.

"My father was partly responsible for the settlement of the West, and I've followed in his footsteps by taking a hand in its development. Therefore, anything that happens in this part of America—for better or for worse—is of interest to me. You might say I make it my business."

"So?" Kung commented politely, and waited for his visitor to continue.

"I'm very fond of the team of financiers, Chet Harris and Wong Ke," he said. "Not only are they old family friends, but it so happens they manage some property that I own. I was naturally quite distressed when Mr. Wong was severely injured in a brutal attack during a recent visit to Portland."

"I heard of the incident," Kung replied blandly. "It was very distressing."

"I wonder," Toby said pleasantly, "if perhaps your distress was caused by the fact that Mr. Wong was merely beaten half to death rather than killed. If he'd been killed outright, there would have been no way to track his attacker. As it happened, the blame for the assault on him is laid completely at your doorstep, Mr. Kung."

The tong leader showed no animosity. "I am sure you realize, Mr. Holt," he said, "that you'd have an exceptionally difficult time proving your allegation in a court of law. Evidence to convict me or my tong is totally lacking."

"You're speaking of evidence presented in the law courts, Mr. Kung, but as you know every bit as well as I do, the West has found it impossible to wait for the long arm of justice to catch up with the development of the country. Again and again we of the West have been forced to take the law into our own hands rather than wait for the courts to act."

"To be sure," Kung Lee replied. "And it is for precisely such reasons that we of the West have found it necessary to defend ourselves. Vigilante justice is all well and good, but those who are falsely accused must be able to stand up in their own defense and drive off their persecutors."

"One of the most fascinating pastimes in this part of the country," Toby replied, "is that of determining who is the persecutor in any given situation. I'm sure that Wong Ke, who almost lost his life as the result of a completely unjustified beating, would insist that he had been the victim, and I must say I agree wholeheartedly."

Kung remained silent.

"There's a more recent case that I find equally fascinating," Toby continued, carefully regarding Kung. "A courier employed by the United States government was shot to death near my Oregon ranch while in the process of delivering some documents intended for my stepfather, General Blake, the commander of the Army of the West. The killer—or someone closely associated with him—subsequently tried to attack my sister and then me in vain attempts to gain control of those documents, which implicate the tong headed by you with the smuggling of opium as well as human beings. For your information, Mr. Kung, those papers have been read by various officials and are now safely in General Blake's headquarters at Fort Vancouver."

Kung Lee stared hard at Toby. "You accuse my subordinates and me of murder and of attempted murder, Mr. Holt. These are exceptionally grave charges. Can you substantiate them?"

Toby smiled lazily. "As I've already told you, Mr. Kung, I have no interest in substantiating them in a law court. I'm not an attorney, and I don't know the legalities involved. Let me just say that I'm satisfied in my own mind that you and your tong are guilty, and that's good enough for me. You started this war. I didn't, but I intend to finish it. Either you'll back off and leave well enough alone, or you're in this for a fight to the finish. I wanted to give you fair warning and to find out for my own satisfaction exactly where you stand. As for your toady yonder," he continued, nodding in the direction of Ho Tai, "I urge you to call him off, or he'll find that he's taken a larger bite than he's capable of digesting."

"You go too far, Holt, and you try my patience." For the first time, a semblance of stridency crept into Kung Lee's voice. "I have tried hard to deal civilly and politely with you. I have tried to warn you to stay within the law, to confine your interests to matters that are truly of concern to you, and to steer clear of affairs that are none of your concern. But you have persisted. You have believed the glowing publicity you've acquired as a result of your fights with savage Indians and with stupid criminals on the frontier. You are prying into serious matters that are none of your business. Very well, if you insist on playing with fire, you'll be burned. You have been warned, Holt, so be on your guard from this time forward." He rose to his feet.

Toby stood at the same moment, and they bowed to each other formally.

Ho Tai's hand closed over the hilt of the knife he carried in his hand. Before he had time to draw it, however, Toby struck with lightning speed. He pulled his knife from his belt, and in the same instant, he threw it with dazzling accuracy. It landed in the wooden paneling of the wall no more than a quarter of an inch from Ho Tai's head.

In the same split second, another knife appeared in his hand, and he threw it with equal speed and force. It cut into the arm of Kung Lee's chair and quivered there.

"There's no need to return those knives, gentlemen," Toby said mildly. "I have plenty of others where they came from. Keep them as souvenirs, and whenever you look at them, think of me." He smiled slightly.

The two Chinese men stared at him in amazement.

Bowing again, Toby deliberately turned his back on the pair and took his leave, walking slowly out of the room. He knew he was taking a terrible risk, and the hair on the back of his head bristled when he realized that a knife well might land in his back at any moment. At the same time, however, he knew of no better way to show his contempt for men who relied on terror and threats to operate their empire.

His gamble paid off. Both Kung Lee and Ho Tai were so stunned that they were incapable of taking advantage of the opportunity that Toby contemptuously handed them as he left the room, descended the stairs, and walked into the street.

But the battle lines had been drawn, the unequal feud had been moved into the open, and the next time the principals met, they would fight to the finish.

V

Tommie Harding was weary as she maintained her lonely, dangerous vigil in the street outside Dugald's Bar. But she grew alert when Captain Kayross and several of his loyal crew members appeared in a dilapidated cart pulled by a workhorse, and she drew farther back into the shadows. Robin Hood still sat on her shoulder, not understanding what was happening and clinging to her as someone who was familiar to him in a strange world.

Meanwhile, both Edward Blackstone and the other male victim lay unconscious, bound and gagged on the cellar floor. Millicent Randall, still propped against the wall, was terrified as she heard Kellerman and Kayross come down the rickety stairs and begin discussing her.

"Here's a fine kettle of fish," Kellerman said. "Yonder is a wench with whom I was having an affair. She got nosy, and her curiosity led her to find out too damned much about me and my business, so

I had to immobilize her several hours ago. I wonder if you have any use for her."

"We'll soon find out," the sea captain said. Approaching her, he held up a lighted candle to get a better look. Millicent would have pulled away from him but was incapable of movement.

Tearing her blouse open with his free hand, Kayross looked at her breasts intently, prodding them as though she were cattle. Then he reached out and gropingly felt her buttocks.

"She's rather dirty and smudged at the moment," he said, "but she looks as though when she's cleaned and properly made up, she can be quite handsome."

"That's right," Kellerman said. "She's a real beauty."

"Her figure is good, and that's important," the captain declared.

"What do you have in mind?" Kellerman asked.

"The imperial viceroy in Canton," Captain Kayross said, "keeps a large harem in his palace there. He's especially partial to white-skinned girls, but they're much more difficult for him to obtain than are Orientals, as you can imagine. Once he hears that this wench is available, he'll pay any price for her. You and I can share a fortune."

"That solves the problem very nicely," Kellerman said.

The captain was lost in thought for a moment or two. "We'll also have to make certain," he finally said, "that she will be cooperative when I present her to the viceroy. She'll have to learn some Eastern customs, like how and when to kowtow."

"She's very bright," Kellerman said sarcastically. "I'm sure she has the ability to learn whatever will be required of her."

"She'll have the entire Pacific crossing to learn," Kayross replied, "and I have just the right instructor for her. If it's all right with you, we'll transfer her to the *Diana* along with the new indentured seamen, and she can begin taking lessons immediately."

"The sooner the better," Kellerman said indifferently. He and the captain mounted the steps, and when they closed the trapdoor behind them, blackness once again enveloped the interior of the cellar.

Mortification, fear, and violent anger suffused Millicent. She had been stupid beyond belief. First she had become involved with Luis de Cordova, and as if she had not suffered enough in that relationship, she had taken up with Karl Kellerman, who was even more brutal and callous in his treatment of her. The prospect of becoming part of a harem filled her with horror and loathing, but she was helpless, unable to escape what appeared to be her certain destiny. Only the remnants of her shredded pride prevented her from weeping, and as she leaned against the cold, damp stones of the cellar wall, she wished that she would awaken and discover that she had merely dreamed the dreadful situation in which she found herself.

Before long, Kayross and Kellerman returned with the Greek members of the ship's crew. Aided

by Kellerman's two henchmen, they carried the unconscious bodies of the men, along with Millicent
Randall, up the stairs and piled them into the horse-
drawn cart. A tarpaulin concealed the captives from
the gaze of any stray passersby who might be abroad
at this very early hour.

The cart, driven by one of Captain Kayross's
crew members, creaked as it moved off through the
silent city. The captain and his remaining men followed on foot close behind it and kept a wary watch
that proved unnecessary. The streets remained silent
and deserted.

Only Tommie Harding was aware of what was
happening. Following the cart at a distance, she was
careful to stay in the shadows at all times. As she
walked, she kept looking for a constable, but no
policemen appeared, nor did anyone else.

The cart rumbled down the cobblestones, and
the thumping of the workhorse's hooves seemed to
obliterate the pounding of Tommie's heart. After
walking for what seemed like a considerable distance,
Tommie marveled at what she had done so far. She
felt certain that her luck would run out at any time
and that her presence would be discovered.

A huge shape loomed up ahead in the murky
night, and although Tommie was thoroughly familiar
with waterfront districts, she was so tired that it
took her several seconds to realize that they had
arrived at the docks and that the bulk was that of a
steam-propelled freighter.

The workhorse halted beside a gangway that was

lowered from the main deck of the vessel to the wharf, and crew members immediately transferred the captives to the ship.

If Tommie had been thinking clearly, she would have marked the name and the exact location of the ship and would have gone off in search of the police. But her long night's vigil had dulled her mind, and she could think only that she had to follow Edward at all costs and know where he was being concealed. Awaiting her opportunity, she sneaked on board and crept behind a mound of cargo lashed to the deck. Looking out from this vantage point, she searched in vain for Edward.

She had no way of knowing that Millicent had been taken to one of the cabins on the upper deck that was reserved for passengers while Edward and the other male prisoner had been taken below to the hold, where they would remain until they regained consciousness. But Tommie knew enough about ships to realize that she could not wander where she pleased in search of Edward. At any moment she could unexpectedly come face to face with one of the officers or seamen.

All at once, a terrible sense of panic assailed her. She had been concentrating so hard on her problem of finding Edward that everything else had been obliterated from her mind, and only now did it occur to her that Robin Hood was no longer perched on her shoulder. The little monkey had vanished since coming on board the freighter.

*   *   *

When Edward Blackstone finally awakened, he was instantly alert. Smelling the stale air and feeling the hard deck beneath his prone body, he knew at once that he was in grave danger. He confirmed this impression when he discovered that his wrists and ankles were bound. An ache at the back of his skull told him that he had probably succumbed to a sharp blow. It was dark in the hold, but the smell of the sea and the slight motion told Edward that he was on board a vessel. He knew also that Karl Kellerman was responsible for his predicament.

Edward found that he had limited mobility but could move his hands up and down several inches. Thus he was able to reach into the hip pocket of his trousers and was infinitely relieved to discover that he still had possession of the small knife that he always kept hidden.

Wedging the open-bladed knife into a crack between two floorboards in the deck, Edward began to press and rub his wrist bonds against the sharp blade.

Suddenly he was startled when something soft landed on his legs, and he looked down to see a small monkey dressed in green perching there. Robin Hood began to chatter delightedly.

Edward had no time to wonder how Robin Hood had gotten there. Moving his wrists up and down against the knife, he continued to saw frantically. Soon the strands of rope began to part, and ultimately they fell away and Edward's arms came free. Quickly removing his gag and untying his legs, Edward picked up the knife and cautioned the monkey to remain silent. Then he looked around. Seeing the other man now awake and cursing as he found himself in the same predicament as Edward's, he cut away his bonds. The man thanked him profusely and said his name was Sam. Edward introduced himself. Meanwhile, Robin Hood leaped up to his accustomed perch on Edward's shoulder.

Neither Edward nor the man he liberated knew why they had been brought to this place, but they were determined to find out. With Edward in the lead, they opened a heavy metal door and found themselves in front of a mammoth furnace, where Wallace Dugald and three other unfortunate wretches were shoveling coal into the open maw of a blazing boiler. All four were chained.

Experimenting swiftly, Edward managed to strike a link on each man's chain with the sharp blade of a heavy metal coal shovel, using such force that the link parted. Thereafter, it was relatively easy to pry the two ends apart and set the imprisoned men free.

Rivers of perspiration cut through the grime of coal dust on Wallace's face and torso as he said in a voice so choked with emotion that it was barely audible, "Thanks be to the Almighty for this deliverance. I thank you, Lord, for hearing my prayer and giving me the chance to even the score with Karl Kellerman. You may hold me to my bargain, Lord: I don't care what becomes of me once I've had the chance to kill him in a way that will repay him for the terrible misery he has caused me. I swear to you, Lord, I won't rest. I'll work day and night until I've obtained vengeance against this evil Kellerman, who is a blot on all that is good, for your sake and in your name. Amen."

Even though it was blazing hot in front of the big furnace, a cold chill crept up Edward's spine as he heard the words of the enraged Scotsman.

Millicent had been shoved into a cabin that at first glance was both spacious and comfortable. It had two portholes that overlooked the Mississippi River and was furnished with a large, bare-mattressed bed, a dressing table amply stocked with cosmetics and perfumes, a table, several chairs, and a chest of drawers.

A Greek crew member had escorted her into the cabin. On his heels was a short Malay woman, slender but wiry, whose age was almost impossible to guess. She was brown-skinned, with dark eyes, and she was dressed in a simple, knee-length garment that stressed her scrawniness. She wore no shoes but seemed to enjoy oversized jewelry, for she had on large hoop earrings, and several massive bracelets. Her head was wrapped in a turban. In her belt she carried a long kris, a sword with a razor-sharp, weighty blade, and in one hand she carried a wooden rod that was about a yard long.

Captain Kayross now appeared and spoke to the woman at length, glancing frequently at Millicent and gesturing toward her as he explained her identity and what he had in mind for her teacher. Listening intently, the Malay woman nodded from time to time. Her eyes gleamed, and a hint of a smile appeared at the corners of her thin lips.

When the captain left, the woman moved swiftly. She took the gag from Millicent's mouth and cut the bonds that tied her ankles together, but left her hands still bound. "You sit!" she commanded, and pointed to the dressing-table stool.

Millicent moved to the seat and sank onto it gratefully. She was extremely weary after her long night of tension and captivity.

The woman went to a cabinet, took a jug from it, and removed the stopper. She lifted the container to her mouth and, after taking a large swallow of the contents, wiped her mouth with the back of her free hand. Then she held the jug up to the prisoner's mouth. "You drink now!" she said. The contents had a nauseating odor, and Millicent's stomach turned over. Unable to use her hands to get rid of the offending jug, she averted her face.

The woman lost patience. Grabbing Millicent's hair, she tugged fiercely, forcing her mouth open, and poured the liquid into her.

Millicent's mouth felt bruised, and the liquid soaked the front of her clothes, but she had to admit that the beverage, whatever it was, gave her a measure of renewed strength.

The Malay woman jerked the prisoner around to face her and began applying makeup. She paused briefly when she was almost finished, and Millicent was stunned when she caught a glimpse of herself in the mirror. Her lips were painted dark red, her eyes were almond-shaped, and her high cheekbones were emphasized with rouge. The overall effect was to give her a distinctly Oriental appearance.

Chuckling to herself, the woman removed her kris from her belt and, slashing with it, cut Millicent's clothes from her body from head to toe. Her attire fell away, leaving her completely naked, and the woman even took her shoes and threw them out the nearest porthole into the Mississippi River.

Then, after deliberately cutting the bonds at Millicent's wrists, the woman stood, went to the cabin door, and unlocked it. "I no keep you tied and locked up here," she said. "You go any time you want go. Many men on board. They catch you and fix plenty good." She exploded in laughter.

Millicent knew that the woman spoke the truth. If she appeared on deck, naked or otherwise, the sailors would be certain to catch and rape her. She was confined to the cabin as surely as she would have been had she still been bound hand and foot and had the door been secured.

The woman stood in front of her with arms folded, the wooden rod in one hand. "You be slave to viceroy," she said. "Now we practice. You be slave, I be viceroy. You kowtow!" She indicated that Millicent was to make physical obeisance before her. Startled and uncertain as to what was expected of her, Millicent started to move slowly.

The Malay woman prodded her viciously with the rod, then began to beat her unmercifully across the buttocks with it. The pain was excruciating. Mil-

licent had no choice but to stretch herself out on the
floor and press her face and body close to the dirty,
foul-smelling rug.

The woman hit her again and again with the
rod. "You kowtow more!" she cried. "More!"

Writhing in pain, Millicent tried to press herself
still deeper into the rug. At last the beating stopped,
and the woman motioned for her to rise.

Her backside throbbing, her whole body aching,
Millicent got to her feet. To her dismay, the Malay
woman again directed her to sit at the dressing table
and submit to having additional makeup put on to
repair the damage where perspiration and contact
with the rug on the floor had smudged and wiped
away some of the cosmetics.

Suddenly the woman jarred her by slapping her
hard across the face. "No move!" she commanded.

Somehow Millicent was able to force herself to
sit very quietly while she submitted to the crude
ministrations. Finally satisfied with what she had
done to the captive's face, the woman chuckled
coarsely as she daubed rouge on Millicent's nipples.
Standing back to study the effect, she pinched the
nipples and then prodded her victim with the rod.
"Now," she said, "you practice kowtow."

Millicent seethed in impotent rage. As she
stretched out on the dirty rug, making her obei-
sances and once again being forced to submit to a
beating, she was filled with a desire to attack and kill
her tormentress. But she knew that her physical
strength was far inferior to that of the Malay woman,

and there was nothing she could do but to keep herself prostrate and accept the punishment.

After a time, the woman grew tired of her sport and pointed her rod to the foot of the bed. "Now you sleep," she ordered.

Millicent was so exhausted that she obeyed and soon fell into a troubled sleep.

The woman moved to the head of the bed, rearranged the pillows there to her satisfaction, and, leaning against them, sat cross-legged as she kept a close watch on her charge.

Robin Kayross paced up and down the bridge of the *Diana* and stared out toward the warehouses of the New Orleans waterfront district, which were barely visible in the early morning darkness. Soon dawn would be breaking, and he had a major decision to make.

He was playing a dangerous game, but he was ahead, and he intended to stay ahead. Realizing there was only one way he could ensure his own safety and that of his ship, he summoned his first mate to the bridge.

"We face a potentially dangerous situation," the captain said. "We have a number of shanghaied American citizens on board, and now we also have an American woman, whom we're going to sell to the viceroy in Canton. The American authorities are inclined to be ruthless in the protection of their citizens, and if they should come on board and inspect the ship, we could be in terrible trouble."

"I've been thinking about the problem, too, and I agree with you, sir," the mate replied. "You and I could be held responsible and spend long terms in jail."

"It seems to me," Captain Kayross said, "that the *Diana* is in too prominent a place for our good. If any one of our captives should manage to get loose on the deck and make a scene, dozens of people on shore might become aware of the commotion and notify the police. We need privacy between now and the time that we set sail for Canton and Hong Kong."

The mate nodded vigorously. "That's my thinking exactly, sir," he said.

"Very well." The captain became crisp. "I've got to go ashore on some urgent personal matters. I want you to move the *Diana* immediately. We have made enough money on the aliens, opium, and cargo we brought here to make a profitable trip back to the Orient, so we can leave this dock permanently. And we have plenty of coal on board. Sail the ship to the delta country of the Mississippi River south of New Orleans. I'm sure you remember the place in the bayous where we anchored last year after we had that trouble with the authorities."

The mate nodded eagerly. "Of course, sir! I'll never forget it. That'll be a perfect spot for us now. The prisoners can shout their heads off there, and the only ones who will hear them will be the alligators and snakes."

"Take no unnecessary risks," Captain Kayross told him. "You'll find the charts for the bayous in the chart room, and I want you to follow them without deviation. I'll join you later in the day, after you've anchored."

"Very good, sir," the mate replied.

"Fortunately," the captain said, "we've kept up the fire in the furnace so we have a head of steam worked up. There's no reason to delay."

"I'll weigh anchor and cast off at once, sir," the mate told him. "Don't you worry, we'll be anchored in the bayou waiting for you whenever you show up."

Deep in the hold of the *Diana*, Edward Blackstone heard the stories of Wallace Dugald and the other men who had been kidnapped and spirited aboard the Greek freighter. At last, the whole picture was clear. Karl Kellerman had abducted the unfortunate men after putting knockout drops in their drinks at Dugald's Bar and then had turned them over to the ship's personnel. The captain of the vessel was intending to utilize the services of these unfortunates as slave labor.

Now that Edward had freed himself as well as the others, however, the picture had changed drastically. There were six desperate men in the hold, including Edward, and all of them were determined to regain their freedom, no matter what the cost.

"We can't just lash out indiscriminately," Edward told the group, having completely forgotten the presence of Robin Hood. "We've got to plan our moves carefully and act accordingly. Our worst handicap is our lack of weapons. All we have among us are a number of metal shovels, various lengths of chain, and my one small knife."

"The Greeks carry pistols," one of the men replied, "and their officers have swords, too."

"How many of them are there in all?" Edward asked crisply.

The others conferred among themselves and finally decided that they had about a dozen active enemies including the captain. They had no way of knowing that Kayross was not on board at the present time.

"Most of the remaining crew," one burly man said, "are either Malays or Lascars. I suspect that they came on board the same way we did and were shanghaied from their homes. They've not only been sympathetic to us, but I have me a hunch they'll desert ship without hesitation. One thing is sure—they won't join in any fight against us."

His comrades agreed heartily.

Edward accepted their word. "That reduces the odds against us appreciably, but we're still handicapped by a lack of weapons. What we'll have to do is lay ambushes for our enemies, one by one, until we gain control of enough weapons to fight on equal terms. What we've got to do right now is to plot the best way to get our hands on some pistols and swords."

They conferred quietly, several of them making impractical suggestions that Edward vetoed. All at once, they became aware of the throbbing of the engine and of tremors in the deck beneath their feet.

"The ship is moving!" Wallace said bitterly. "We must be putting out to sea!"

"Maybe, but maybe not," a thin, tall man declared. "I know every inch of the waters around New Orleans. Come with me, Dugald, and we'll see for ourselves." He and Wallace crept away while the rest remained in the hold.

After a wait that seemed interminable, the party heard soft footsteps approaching the hold. Firm grips were taken on shovels and chains.

"Who's there?" Edward called softly.

"We're back!" said one of the returning pair, and the others breathed more easily as the two men came into the room.

"The freighter," the man who knew the Mississippi said, "sure isn't following the main channel that empties into the Gulf of Mexico, so wherever we're headed, we aren't going very far. Most of the other channels end in swamps or feed into lakes in the bayou country."

The rest of the group felt vastly relieved that the freighter was moving into a sparsely settled region of the Mississippi delta rather than out to sea.

All the same, Edward reasoned, it would be wrong to delay. The group's greatest natural advantage, that of surprise, would be lost if they waited too long. His comrades agreed to initiate action as soon as possible.

Although Edward was unfamiliar with the particulars of this vessel's layout, he knew enough about ships in general to make a rough plan, and the others agreed to it without discussion. Only Wallace commented.

"If Karl Kellerman is on board," he said, "he's mine. I don't want anybody else killing or injuring him by accident. I reserve the right to end his life myself!"

One of the first party to have been shanghaied led the group to a passageway that extended from the hatch to the entrance of the furnace room. "Sooner or later," he said, "they're sure to send a couple of men down to make certain that we're feeding the furnace."

Edward silently stationed his comrades on both sides of the narrow passageway, cautioning each of them to maintain absolute quiet until the signal was given that they could talk. Tensely they settled down to await the arrival of foes. Their inability to see clearly in the dark passageway, combined with the vibration of the moving ship, contributed to the mounting tension.

The vigil seemed unending. For what felt like a very long time, the freighter kept up a somewhat better than moderate speed. Then the engine slowed down, and the vibrations eased up. Shortly thereafter, a lighted lantern moved down the passageway, and voices were heard in the distance.

"The coal stokers," one voice said in disgust, "are the laziest swine who have ever sailed the seven seas."

"If they've allowed the fire in the furnace to die down," the other said, "they'll deserve a beating. And they shall have it. I'll personally whip every last mother's son of them."

The footsteps came closer, and the light in the passageway edged steadily nearer.

The victims of abduction scarcely dared to breathe for fear that the slightest sound or motion would reveal their presence prematurely.

Crouching between two large crates of cargo on the main deck of the *Diana*, Tommie was stiff, sore, hungry, and weary. She realized she had made a major mistake in blindly following Edward when he had been carried, unconscious, aboard the freighter, and now she was trapped. She assumed that at least one guard was on duty to keep watch on the cargo, and if she stood upright or moved, she would be seen and would meet Edward's fate. Somehow their futures were bound together.

All of a sudden, something landed on Tommie's shoulder, startling her, and she looked up quickly to see Robin Hood perched there. Delighted that he had returned safely to her, she patted him, and he began to chatter quickly.

At the same time, the ship's engine was turned on, and the whole freighter vibrated. The sound, fortunately, was loud enough that it obliterated the soft noises made by the little monkey.

Suddenly Tommie noted that there was a smudge

of coal dust on the animal's little coat and another on
his feathered hat.

Carefully brushing off the garments, she murmured, "Where on earth have you been, Robin? Oh,
if you could only talk!" The monkey appeared to be
shaking, and the thought occurred to the young woman
that he might be frightened.

Now, to Tommie's horror, the ship had moved
from the dock into the open Mississippi River and
headed slowly downstream. The first thought that
occurred to her was that the vessel had started a
voyage to some distant port. In consternation, she
knew that her presence on board surely would be
discovered after a day or two at sea. She had done
nothing to help Edward, who was still a prisoner of
the ship's crew. All she had succeeded in doing was
to ensure that she, too, would be captured.

Ultimately, Tommie's familiarity with riverboats
restored her common sense, and she grew calmer.
Peering through a narrow space between the crates,
she could see that the freighter was no longer navigat-
ing on the principal route of the Mississippi River
but had turned into a small channel. Dwellings and
other signs of human habitation disappeared from
the banks of the river, and the countryside became
increasingly desolate. From what she knew of the
geography of the region, Tommie reasoned that the
ship was moving into the remote and uninhabitable
swampy country known as the bayous.

It was a relief to realize that the ship's master
was not putting out to sea. At the same time, Tom-

mie knew that the freighter was leaving civilization behind and that wherever it might be going, she would have to rely on herself to come to Edward's aid.

The insistent prodding of the wooden rod awakened Millicent, and she instantly became aware, too, of the ship's motion, but she had no chance to think about the fact that the ship was under way. The Malay woman, sitting cross-legged at the opposite end of the bed, was reclining against pillows and grinning evilly at her.

"You practice kowtow! Now!" the woman commanded.

Half-asleep, Millicent dragged herself off the bed and made an obeisance. She had anticipated a blow with the rod, but nevertheless it was a shock when the woman struck her hard. Her rage mounting with each blow she received, Millicent was nevertheless compelled to endure the torment until the Malay woman stopped because her arm was growing tired.

"Now you sleep!" she commanded.

Tired, battered, and bruised, Millicent painfully climbed back into bed and soon fell asleep again.

Too late, a length of chain clanked its dismal warning as Edward brought it down full force onto the head of the unsuspecting ship's officer. The man staggered forward a step or two and crumpled to the deck, dying without making a sound.

Wallace accorded the same treatment to the other mate, and he, too, died silently. There was no need for any assistance from the other shanghaied men.

The refugees obtained a rich harvest of weapons. The two officers had been carrying three pistols and two swords, which the shanghaied men eagerly appropriated. In addition, they took the lantern, which would prove useful to them in the critical time ahead.

Edward was the only member of the group who knew how to use a sword, so he helped himself to one of the blades. The other he gave to Wallace, who took it but insisted on keeping his chain, also. "I'll be able to do double damage," he muttered, his anger unassuaged by the action he had already seen.

Believing that the arms they had acquired helped to equalize the odds that had been so much against them, the group surged upward. They came to a closed hatch directly overhead, accessible by means of a ladder attached to a bulkhead. Edward halted beneath the hatch and beckoned his comrades to gather closely around him. "When we move into the open, lads," he said, "don't bunch together. You'll make too tempting and too good a target. Spread out and take cover wherever you find it. We'll move quickly, with the men who've acquired arms leading the way. Wherever you see an opponent, cut him down quickly and without mercy. Then, make certain you help yourselves to any weapons he may be carrying and share them with your companions. I'll do my best to keep all of you within sight, and as our fight develops, I'll try to issue any additional instructions that might be needed." Without further ado, he climbed the ladder and cautiously pushed the hatch open. None of the ship's personnel appeared to be within sight, and the entire group scrambled into the open behind him without being detected.

Edward discovered that they were far aft on a deck that contained boxes and cases of cargo. He waved his companions to port and starboard. As they started to advance cautiously toward the prow of the freighter, two Greek seamen and a pair of Malay sailors—who were about to prove themselves loyal to Captain Kayross—appeared in the open.

It was unnecessary for Edward to order an attack. He and his men surged forward, making the quartet the objects of their hatred and frustration. Wielding chains and shovels with abandon, they assaulted the startled seamen. The pistols were ready for instant use when circumstances made their use feasible.

No force could have contained Wallace, who was endowed with a maniacal strength as he hacked wildly with his sword and wielded his chain with equal abandon. His rage was so great it shook him to the core, almost consuming him. He was determined to even the score with every last one of his tormentors.

Edward was equally outraged, but he relied on his skills developed over a period of years rather than on brute strength. The sword he had acquired became an extension of his right arm as he slashed and cut with it, wielding it with such grace and rapidity that it was almost impossible for the men at whom its aim was directed to halt it.

A thrust aimed at an opponent's throat found its target, and another blow almost decapitated one of the Malays. In all, Edward accounted for three of the enemy in a matter of seconds, while Wallace clumsily but effectively disposed of the fourth.

Edward took another pair of pistols from the dead men, which he gave to two of his comrades. Then, leaving the bodies of the dead where they had fallen, he waved his group forward. The brief encounter had created more of a commotion than Edward and his men realized, and other seamen and officers began to gather amidships. Somewhat to Edward's surprise, there were a number of Malays and Lascars in this group as well, along with the Greeks. He had been wrong to believe that the Malays and Lascars would automatically fall in with his own group; obviously their loyalty was with Captain Kayross because he paid their wages.

In almost no time, a battle was raging. The shanghaied men ducked behind crates and boxes in order to protect themselves from the pistols of their foes, and the crew members did the same.

Edward knew it was imperative that his men maintain the momentum they had achieved. "Keep moving, lads. Keep moving forward!"

The shanghaied men, inspired by his example and thirsting for revenge, continued to press, step by step, toward the prow of the ship. The air was filled with bullets now as shots were freely exchanged.

Edward's colleagues were strangers from different walks of life. They were united only by the fact that they had suffered a common personal catastrophe, but their anger at their treatment had given them the courage of lions. They responded like military veterans to Edward's orders to keep their heads down in order to avoid enemy sniper fire, and they carefully conserved their ammunition, firing their pistols only when they had clear targets.

There was a brief lull in the exchange of gunfire, and to Edward's astonished dismay, a blond head appeared above the tops of the crates that separated the two forces. Tommie Harding stood upright with Robin Hood clinging to one shoulder.

Edward had no idea how she happened to be on board the freighter, and although now he knew why the little monkey had appeared out of nowhere, this was not the time to ask for explanations. "Tommie!" he called. "Get down and stay down! Don't expose yourself to crossfire!"

She obeyed at once, smiling broadly when she heard his voice. She remained hidden between two crates, rejoicing because she knew Edward was safe.

Edward's voice reached her again. "We're moving past your position," he called. "Make no attempt to follow us—stay in concealment. I'll let you know when it's safe for you to come out into the open."

Again, pistol shots were exchanged by the two forces, and the little monkey on Tommie's shoulder began to tremble violently. She stroked him reassuringly. "Don't worry, Robin," she whispered. "Edward has taken charge, so everything is going to be all right."

Raving and cursing as he advanced, Wallace continued to press forward, waving his sword and seemingly impervious to enemy bullets. His ferocity and anger served to goad the other shanghaied men, and they pressed forward, too. At Edward's insistence, their advance was cautious. He was taking no chances.

As he dashed from one row of crates to the next, Edward unexpectedly came upon two men, a Malay and a Lascar, who were crouching behind the nearest box. With his sword he quickly disposed of them.

He found that the pair had been carrying clumsy, British-made weapons that were copies of Colt repeating pistols. Nevertheless, he was grateful for the acquisition of still more firearms, and he kept the pistols for his own use. By this time, every member of the little band carried arms, and Edward was convinced that they could look after themselves.

A bullet plowed up a furrow in the planking of the deck only inches from the spot where Edward was crouching. The enemy's aim was far too accurate for comfort, and he searched for his foe.

All at once, he saw that the Greek first mate of the *Diana* was standing on the bridge of the ship and taking aim at him again. Sighting the officer down the barrel of the cumbersome pistol, Edward pulled the trigger.

Ordinarily he was a superb shot, but the weapon was faulty, and his bullet lodged in the mate's shoulder. However, the officer dropped his pistol to the deck and grasped his shoulder. He shouted out something to the crew that Edward could not make out.

Just then, the young Englishman realized that a retreat was under way. The mate and the other Greeks who formed the nucleus of the crew raced to the starboard side of the vessel, where they lowered the ship's gig into the water and hastily climbed down a rope ladder hanging over the side of the vessel into the boat.

As Edward and his companions ran to the railing on the starboard side of the freighter, the Malays and Lascars, including both those who had been loyal to Captain Kayross and those who wanted no part in the combat, leaped to the rail and plunged into the swampy waters of the cove, where the vessel was now riding at anchor.

The ship's gig made steady progress toward the shore, as the Greek crew members bent over the oars. While Edward and Wallace stood side by side at the rail, watching in fascinated horror, alligators materialized from several parts of the cove and began to bear down on the men who were swimming with all their strength toward the shore. The huge creatures resembled half-submerged logs as they drew nearer to the fleeing seamen.

The alligators opened their huge jaws, and the waters became bloody as they went after arms and legs. The air was filled with the screams of the helpless, dying men. As the churning, foaming waters turned red, a slow chill ascended Edward's spine, and he rubbed his arms vigorously. "May God have mercy on their souls," he muttered.

At his direction, Wallace led their comrades in search of another ship's boat, which they found near the stern. They lowered it with difficulty into the waters of the bayou, and when that task was completed, Edward called to Tommie that it was safe for her now to reappear. She stood and moved toward him slowly, her gait unsteady.

As Edward reached for her and took her into his arms, Robin Hood jumped from her shoulder to his, chattering wildly. As the monkey continued to express his opinion of all that had happened, Edward and Tommie, oblivious to the presence of the remaining men, embraced and kissed.

Millicent Randall was prodded awake frequently and ordered by the Malay woman, "Now you kowtow!" Regardless of whether she moved rapidly or slowly, she was beaten for her pains and was forced to suffer still another beating as she kowtowed. The cruelty of the woman was unbearable.

One time when Millicent was awakened, she distinctly heard the sounds of pistol fire and shouts on the deck. She looked across at the Malay woman, but her captor seemed to be paying no attention to the commotion. Suddenly Millicent froze.

The woman was dozing on the pillows at the head of the bed. She had slumped on them, and her kris had fallen out of her belt and was lying beside her.

Scarcely aware of what she was doing, yet at the same time realizing that she was being given an unexpected opportunity to escape, Millicent reached out and grasped the handle of the sword.

At that instant the Malay woman opened her eyes. Instantly wide awake, she reached with both hands for the length of steel, unmindful of the fact that the double-edged blade was razor sharp.

The kris sliced into the palms of her hands and the insides of her fingers, causing her to bleed profusely, but she tightened her hold.

Seeing the pain and the hatred in the woman's glittering eyes, Millicent instinctively tightened her hold and pulled harder. The woman responded by tightening her own grip, causing her hands to bleed still more heavily as she tried to wrest the deadly blade from her captive. The pain that the woman suffered was excruciating, but she withstood it in silence, and her grip firm, she exerted all her strength as she continued to pull the deadly sword toward her. Beads of sweat appeared on her forehead, and rivulets ran down her face, but she ignored them, just as she ignored the blood spurting from her hands.

Struggling with all of her inferior might, Millicent noted that the point of the kris's blade was aimed directly at the body of her tormentor and was on her left side in the middle of her chest. It was about a half-inch from her body. Suddenly a horrible idea occurred to Millicent, and she knew she had to utilize it. She, who had never committed any deed that had caused physical injury to another human being, no longer had a choice. If she failed to act immediately, she would be made to pay dearly.

The rage that had been building within her decided the issue, and without giving the matter further consideration, she released her grip on the handle.

The Malay woman had been tugging at the blade with all of her might, and she could not lighten her efforts in that split second after Millicent released her hold. The woman's force behind her deadly grip plunged the blade deep within her own body. Collapsing over the kris, she fell dead onto the bed.

Millicent gasped. Never had she seen death so close. As for the Malay woman herself, Millicent felt neither compassion nor pity. The woman had chosen to live violently, and now she had died violently.

Of more immediate concern was Millicent's need to escape. She went over to the Malay woman and hastily began to unwind the turban, which was made of soft silk. She was gratified to discover that there was yard after yard of it, long enough, she knew, to be wrapped in some way around her body. First, however, she had to get out of the cabin. Hastening to the door, Millicent listened carefully and could hear the sounds of the battle raging on deck. Not knowing what was taking place but fearful she would get into more difficulty if she exposed herself, she opened the door cautiously and crept to a pile of crates. Finding that one was partially empty, she hid herself in it, prepared to bide her time until it was safe to come out.

*　　*　　*

It was the urgent desire of the entire company to put as much distance between themselves and the *Diana* as possible, but there was one thing they still had to do: find Millient Randall, since Tommie was sure she had also been brought onto the ship. But after splitting up and searching the entire vessel, Edward and his men found no trace of her, only the cut-up body of the Malay woman, whose death was a total mystery. There was nothing more they could do and so two of the men descended into the ship's boat, which they held steady while Tommie slowly went down to it, going hand over hand down the rope ladder. Edward Blackstone was the last member of the group to reach the boat, and as he picked up a pair of oars, his comrades did the same. Tommie sat in the prow with her back to it, the monkey perched on her shoulder as the men rowed toward the shore. The vessel cut through the water, and to the relief of everyone present, the alligators kept their distance.

At last the shore loomed directly ahead, and several of the men leaped from the boat onto dry land, then pulled the craft after them. The boat the Greek crew members had used to make their escape was beached nearby on the shore, but there was no sign of the men. No doubt they had fled in the direction of New Orleans.

Edward stepped ashore, then picked up Tommie and deposited her on the ground. "If my sense of direction hasn't failed me," he said to the assembled group, "New Orleans is due north of here. But I'm afraid we have a walk of a considerable distance before we get back into the city."

"That's all right," Tommie replied. "We're safe and we're together, and nothing else matters."

With one accord, the group headed toward New Orleans. They reached the waterfront district shortly after noon and went directly to Dugald's Bar, which, as Edward had anticipated, was closed and locked for the day. There was no sign of Captain Kayross or Kellerman or, more importantly, Millicent.

"I suggest that all of us go home," Wallace said, "and that we plan to meet back here later this evening, say around midnight. We have a score to settle with Kellerman, and I'm not abdicating my right to be the first to put a bullet into him!"

"Not until he tells us what has become of my cousin," Edward put in.

They went their separate ways, with Edward and Tommie heading for their hotel. When they reached it, they found no sign of Jim Randall or Randy Savage, and they went to their rooms and changed their clothes, then had a meal in the dining room, the first food they had eaten in almost twenty-four hours. Then they went upstairs again. By this time, the couple had exchanged information fully, with Tommie explaining how she had happened to be on board the freighter when the fight erupted.

"Didn't you realize the risks involved?" Edward demanded. "Didn't you know you were taking a terrible chance with your own life?"

"You were in danger," she replied, "and I didn't stop to think of anything else."

When they reached their rooms, they found that Jim and Randy were still out. Robin Hood, whom they had left in the parlor of the suite while they dined, was exhausted and sound asleep on the sofa. They left some fruit that they had obtained from the dining room on a small table next to the sofa. Then they stood for a moment or two, looking at each other. "I'll have quite a story," Edward said, "to pass on to our children and grandchildren."

"I was so concerned about you," Tommie replied, "that I didn't stop to think of myself or of the danger I might be in until bullets started flying. But I guess I acted stupidly," she went on. "I wanted to help, and I tried to help, but I succeeded only in getting in the way and then making your job more difficult. I should have had faith in you and known that you'd be able to escape."

"The fact was," Edward began slowly, "that you cared about my welfare more than your own." He put his hands on her shoulders and looked deeply into her eyes. "We've been betrothed long enough. It's time we get married."

"I agree," Tommie said, "but we can't marry unless my father gives us his blessing. I have no doubt he will, but unless we can intercept him by telegram, we would have to wait until he reached the headwaters of the Missouri River, turned the *Big Muddy* around, and sailed back to St. Louis. So, tomorrow, we'll start trying to reach him at one of the regular stops."

"You get into such trouble when you're left to your own devices," he said, "that it's very difficult to wait. Unfortunately, I agree with you, however, and we won't be married until your father comes back to St. Louis and then, I hope, to New Orleans. The moment he gets here, you're going to become my wife."

There was no need for words, and Tommie just nodded. They continued to look at each other, and suddenly their patience snapped. They were wrapped in each other's arms, and their kiss became increasingly passionate, increasingly demanding.

They wanted each other badly, and that aphrodisiac overcame the exhaustion and the uncertainties that they had suffered the last twenty-four hours. Out of consideration for Tommie's father, they could not be married until he formally gave them his blessing and was present for the ceremony, but they had succeeded in winning their gamble with death and felt there was only one way they could celebrate their victory.

They moved to Tommie's bedchamber, where they quickly undressed and embraced again on the bed. Now they felt only an overwhelming desire that swept all else to one side, and their lovemaking became increasingly frenzied. With the absolute honesty of two people in love, they cast aside all pretense and freely gave of themselves.

When Edward took Tommie, she clung to him,

and they soared to a mutual climax that seemed to last forever and that left both of them utterly limp, totally exhausted and spent. The events of the previous night had taken a heavier toll than they knew, and they fell sound asleep in each other's arms.

When Jim and Randy returned to the suite that day, having gone out looking for the missing Edward and Tommie, they were greeted by an excited Robin Hood. The monkey chattered at the two men long and rapidly. They soon discovered that Tommie and Edward had returned safely from their adventure, and they curbed their curiosity until the following morning, when the couple awakened in time for breakfast and a conference, at which Jim and Randy were told the entire story.

After what seemed like an eternity of waiting, Millicent realized that all sounds of the battle had ceased. She opened the lid of the crate, and seeing no one, she crept out, carrying the long turban cloth in her hand.

The ship seemed deserted, but suddenly she halted and gasped. The body of a dead Malay seaman was crumpled a short distance from her down the deck. In the next few minutes, Millicent discovered two more bodies on the decks, and her brain reeling, she decided that the freighter was a death ship. She searched in vain for a boat that would take her ashore, and it finally dawned on her that the boats had disappeared when the living had fled.

She was not particularly superstitious, but the

stench of death was in her nostrils and contributed to her feeling of hysteria. Looking across the expanse of water toward the trees that lined the shore, she knew only that she had to leave the *Diana* or lose her mind.

She was an excellent swimmer, thanks to the childhood summers she had spent on the shores of Chesapeake Bay. Quickly wrapping the turban around her head, to keep the material from getting wet, she climbed down the rope ladder and dived into the bayou, striking out for the shore, her strokes long and powerful.

Only when she was able to stand in knee-deep water and was making her way ashore did she glance over her shoulder, and not until she saw two half-submerged "logs" drifting rapidly toward her did she realize the danger she was in. Those logs were mammoth alligators, and in her panic, she fled up to the shore and retreated a considerable distance into the woods before she paused for breath. To her infinite relief, the alligators had not followed her, and she knew she was safe.

At last she was able to devote her attention to her appearance. She removed the turban from her head and then wound it loosely around her body, beginning at the calves of her legs and working upward. After winding it several times around her breasts, she brought it up over her shoulders and was relieved to find that it even covered the upper portion of her arms. Millicent's feet were still bare, but she had no way of obtaining shoes.

Now a much greater problem faced her. She had no idea where she was or how she would get back to New Orleans. She would just have to trudge through the jungles of the bayou country until she found someone or something that would show her the way.

Still, her luck had been good so far: She was free of the Malay woman's torture, and she had escaped a fate as a concubine in the harem of an Oriental potentate. She would find the strength to walk barefooted all the way back to New Orleans, even if it took her many days.

VI

A cool breeze blew through the open sides of the stone gazebo in the spacious rear yard behind the sedate New Orleans home. In the gazebo was a large reclining chair with a small table set up on either side of it. On each table a game of dominoes was in progress. The middle-aged Domino, his color restored to a normal, healthy hue, a small bandage on his head, sat in the chair, playing dominoes with two of his associates simultaneously.

"These bones," he said, "are doing exactly what I want them to do today." He turned from one table to the other, picking up the oblongs of ivory and manipulating them with ease as he moved first against one and then the other of his associates. The gang members, at best bored by the game, played dutifully. Both of them knew that Domino was cheating, but they also knew better than to complain.

Conversation was limited to the requirements of the game. Occasionally one or another player would call "Go!" and his opponent would immediately take up the challenge. Eventually the convalescing man would cry "Domino!" and that particular game would end in another victory for him.

He did not mind in the least that his cheating enabled him to win. Victory for its own sake was his goal, and his triumphant "Domino!" was the only talk that mattered.

Eventually Domino grew tired of the game. Taking a thick watch from a waistcoat pocket, he glanced at it, then turned to his underlings. "I'm expecting a visit," he said, "from a wench who works in one of our brothels. Send her in to me when she gets here, please."

The pair exchanged a quick look. "Oh, she's been here for some time," one of the men replied. "We've been waiting until we finished playing before telling you."

Domino lost his temper. "When will you boys ever learn that time is money?" he demanded. "Send her out to me right now! And stay around. We'll play a few more games after I'm finished with her."

The pair exchanged another look as one of them quickly rose to his feet and hurried off to the main house. Apparently they had been mistaken in their assumption of the purpose for which their employer wanted the prostitute.

The man reappeared shortly, leading across the lawn a heavily made-up blonde. Her skirt fitted her so tightly that her hips rolled as she walked, and every male within eyesight, including several guards stationed on the premises, watched her with obvious pleasure. "I thought you forgot all about me, honey," she said to Domino, a hint of complaint in her voice.

He shook his head, then growled at her, "I was just now told you were here. Sit down!"

She sat in a chair that one of the men had vacated, and a slit appeared at one side of her skirt to display a svelte leg encased in a black lace stocking.

"You know who I am?" Domino demanded.

"Sure," she replied. "All the girls in the house know that you're the big boss."

"Do you know why you're here?"

She was surprised. "Well, no, not exactly, but I thought—"

"Leave the thinking to me," Domino told her brutally. "You'll stay out of trouble that way. All right, my dear, let's take a look at you."

The woman knew what was expected of her. She rose to her feet, slowly ran her hands down the front of her body, then raised her skirt high above her knees and lowered it again, inch by inch.

"You'll do," Domino said candidly, and waved her back to her chair. "I expect you know how to get a man interested in you."

"I've yet to meet one who will run away," she replied confidently.

Domino liked her. He grinned, and she returned his smile boldly. "I have a job for you," he said, "a very simple job. Do you know a man named Karl Kellerman?"

She shook her head. "No, sir."

"He's tall, and he isn't bad looking, and he thinks he's irresistible to women."

"I know the type," she said, her distaste evident in her voice.

"I want you to snag him, take him to an apartment that I'll have set up for you, and then go to bed with him. That's all there is to it. Some of my boys will show up, and the instant they appear, you're to grab your clothes and get out. That's the end of it."

The blonde was astonished. "That's all you want me to do?"

Domino was maddeningly calm. "That's all," he assured her with a steady smile.

The woman was confused. "But why—"

"No questions, please!" Domino said sharply. "The less you know, the fewer questions you'll have to answer and the safer you'll be. I hope I make myself clear."

There was a long pause in the conversation while the woman pondered his words. "Very clear," she said at last.

He removed several bills from a large wad that he carried in a pocket. "Here's one hundred dollars," he said. "Come back after you've done the job, and there'll be another hundred waiting for you. In the meantime, get it into your head that you've never come near this place, you've never set eyes on me, and you've never held a conversation with me."

The woman took the money, folded it, and raising her skirt, deposited it in the top of her stocking.

"I'm glad to see you at last, honey," she said sweetly. "I've never met you before, but it's a real pleasure."

Domino chuckled appreciatively. "Eddie," he said to one of his underlings, "take her to Charlie. He'll give her the key to the apartment and will fill her in on the details of where she can make contact with Kellerman."

Watching the swivel-hipped woman as she made her way to the main house with his subordinate, Domino nodded his head in pleasant anticipation. His men would trap Kellerman in the apartment and then slowly, brutally put him to death. It was time for Kellerman to suffer the tortures of the damned for what he had done.

Karl Kellerman's streak of good luck seemed unending. That night at his favorite gaming and dining club, he had more than quadrupled his original evening's wager. Knowing nothing of the events aboard the *Diana* earlier in the day, he was looking forward to meeting Captain Robin Kayross later that night for the last time and collecting the balance of the money for the shanghaied recruits, whom he had delivered to the Greek sea captain in the early hours of the morning. In the meantime, he had not only rid himself permanently of Millicent Randall but would be paid a great deal of money for her after she was turned over to the Chinese viceroy in Canton. Now the blonde he had met earlier in the evening, the woman who had brought him good luck by sitting beside him at the gaming table, had invited him back

to her apartment with her that evening, an invitation
he had accepted with alacrity.

Now, he studied her over the rim of his wineglass.
"If you knew me better," he said, "you might have
thought twice about that invitation."

The blonde moved closer to him and pressed
her leg against him. "Why is that?" she asked
demurely.

He smiled faintly. "Although I'm fairly new in
town," he said, "I've already acquired a reputation
that does a lady's name no good."

"I'm willing to risk it," she replied, flirting with
him over the top of her glass.

He drained his wine, picked up the bottle, and
refilled both their glasses.

As the blonde raised her glass, returning his
silent toast, she reflected that she had never earned
the enormous sum of two hundred dollars so easily.
It had been a simple matter to meet Kellerman and
to arouse his interest in her. Now he had accepted
her invitation to accompany her to the apartment,
and the rest of the evening would be sure to go
according to plan, too. Then she would be paid the
second hundred dollars. She had no idea whether
Domino merely planned to embarrass Kellerman or
whether his intent was more sinister, but she had no
intention of finding out. Several of the girls at the
brothel had assured her that Domino was the most
important gang leader in New Orleans and that his
influence was as widespread as his reputation for
ruthless behavior. He was treating her fairly, with

great generosity, and she wanted to return the favor, to do as good a job as she possibly could for him.

After they finished their light supper, Kellerman hesitated for a moment at the gaming tables.

His companion took his arm. "Don't play again," she murmured. "Your luck has been too good tonight and might change."

He nodded. Her advice made sense.

"Besides," she went on in a still lower, sexy tone, "I think we have things to do that will be far more exciting than gambling."

He thrilled to the promise in her voice and, turning away, accompanied her down the stairs.

Kellerman hired a closed carriage and driver, and he and the blonde sat close together on the plush seat, kissing whenever the carriage moved through a park or down a particularly dark thorough-fare. At last the driver deposited them in front of the building in which the woman allegedly occupied the apartment on the second floor, a suite of rooms that had a large balcony overlooking a parklike area. As she searched in her handbag for the key to the flat, she caught a glimpse of several dark figures loitering behind a clump of bushes growing across the street. Domino's men were already in place, waiting for her signal, which would bring them hurrying to the apartment.

When the couple reached the apartment, which the woman had visited previously, she mixed Keller-man a stiff drink of whiskey before disappearing into the bedroom to change into a negligee and high-

heeled slippers. Following her detailed instructions
to the letter, she placed her own attire in a neat pile
near the door so she could snatch her clothes, change
quickly, and leave the place at once when the time
came for her to vanish.

Kellerman was reclining on a divan in the living
room; he had drained his drink, and his boots were
resting on the floor beside him.

The woman refilled his glass, then stood in front
of him until he took the hint and swept her into his
arms. She allowed her negligee to fall open, and she
let him caress her nude body as he pleased. When
she was certain that he was aroused, she murmured
the suggestion that they adjourn to the bedchamber.

As Kellerman turned away, accepting her invitation, she clutched her robe together and stepped out
onto the balcony for a moment, where she yawned
and stretched. This was her signal to Domino's
accomplices, notifying them that she and their victim
were now going to bed and that they could break in.

When she joined him in the bedchamber, she
saw that he was still dressed except for his boots and
that he was glaring at her suspiciously.

"What the hell was the meaning of that?" he
demanded roughly. "What the hell were you doing?"

A sudden fear gripping her, she shrank from
him. "I—I don't know what you're talking about."

"When you went out to that balcony just now,
you were signaling to somebody, I swear it."

A vice of terror gripped her heart. "I don't know

ted. "You're

ing   t a lot of
                staying
        he uth—

who to a
        he
ded,   e, he ss of
    and he has ap-
wn coin. He felt ain
necessary to do to he r
e wondered who coul
, he re Perhaps he would never

tered the streets of the work-
llerman reflected that what he
was true. He was tough and
y of money, and he managed
of his enemies.

ed Dugald's Bar, Kellerman
ng him generously. Then he
oor and entered the building,
. The sign in the window said
how Kellerman wanted it, for
oss was to be in private.

g to wait before the breathless,
Kayross, accompanied by three
showed up. Refusing Keller-

barking of watchd
were aroused by the
busy thoroughfare, an
sank into it after first
Dugald's Bar, where
tain Kayross anyway.

His luck, he deci
he had escaped intact
erous woman in her o
what he had found it
deserved her fate. H
hired her to set him up.
know.

As the carriage e
ing man's district, Ke
had told the blonde
resilient, he had plen
to stay one step ahead

When they reach
paid the driver, tippi
unlocked the tavern d
which was eerily quiet
Closed, and that was
his meeting with Kayr

He didn't have lon
nervous-looking Robin
of his crew members,
man's offer of a drink
ship's captain launched
taken place earlier tha
had learned about whe

wl
fe
it,
w
b
r

b
w
b
i
h
t
g
l
a
l

what you're talking about," she repeated. "You're imagining things."

"Like hell I am," he replied. "I've got a lot of enemies, and the way I confound them is by staying one step ahead of them. Either tell me the truth—fast—or suffer the consequences."

She was so frightened she could say nothing. Kellerman reached out and caught hold of her by one wrist. As he did, he heard the front door of the apartment open cautiously. His suspicions were confirmed!

Not wasting an instant, he reached into his belt, where he carried a double-edged knife, and with no feeling whatever, he slashed the woman's throat with it, cutting her from ear to ear. As she toppled backward onto the bed, he stooped down, picked up his boots with his free hand, and still clutching the knife, raced out onto the balcony.

Knowing he had no choice, he leaped off the balcony into a clump of bushes below. He landed with a jarring jolt that caused him to drop his knife, but he picked it up instantly. Wiping the blood from it onto the ground and putting it back into his belt, he sprinted in his stockinged feet toward the trees that beckoned at the far side of the yard. When he gained the temporary sanctuary, he pulled on his boots, reasoning that the death of the woman in the apartment should give him a brief respite. But he knew that within seconds, the chase would be on.

He beat a hasty, blind retreat across the yard and through alleyways between houses, ignoring the

barking of watchdogs and the cries of people who
were aroused by their pets. Eventually he came to a
busy thoroughfare, and hailing a passing carriage, he
sank into it after first giving the driver the address of
Dugald's Bar, where he was supposed to meet Captain Kayross anyway.

His luck, he decided, was still good. Once again
he had escaped intact, and he had repaid the treach-
erous woman in her own coin. He felt no remorse for
what he had found it necessary to do to her; she had
deserved her fate. He wondered who could have
hired her to set him up. Perhaps he would never
know.

As the carriage entered the streets of the working man's district, Kellerman reflected that what he
had told the blonde was true. He was tough and
resilient, he had plenty of money, and he managed
to stay one step ahead of his enemies.

When they reached Dugald's Bar, Kellerman
paid the driver, tipping him generously. Then he
unlocked the tavern door and entered the building,
which was eerily quiet. The sign in the window said
Closed, and that was how Kellerman wanted it, for
his meeting with Kayross was to be in private.

He didn't have long to wait before the breathless,
nervous-looking Robin Kayross, accompanied by three
of his crew members, showed up. Refusing Kellerman's offer of a drink to calm him down, the Greek
ship's captain launched into an account of all that had
taken place earlier that day on the *Diana*, which he
had learned about when his surviving crew members